I went to my room and put on two of everything: two pairs of socks and two shirts and two pairs of pants. I crammed my polka-dot necktie into my back pants pocket and took out my nice green-plaid sports jacket that always cheered me up when I saw myself in the mirror, and hung it over a chair so that it would be ready the next morning. I didn't bother about anything else because I wanted to travel light. I planned to sleep in my clothes and slip out quietly the next morning before anybody woke up, because I wasn't going to sign any register as if I was on parole from a prison. I was going to leave for good, without looking back, burning my britches, like they say.

Once in bed, I pulled the blankets up to my neck so that my clothes wouldn't be seen if someone happened to come in. For the first time in weeks, sleep came like a soft hand stroking me, and I slept with a sweetness all around me.

ROBERT CORMIER

• • • • • • • • • • • • • • • •

Take Me Where the Good Times Are

In Memory Of
Frank L Forker
1955 – 1995

Published by
Dell Publishing
a division of
Bantam Doubleday Dell Publishing Group, Inc.
666 Fifth Avenue
New York, New York 10103

The trademark Laurel-Leaf Library® is reigstered in the U.S. Patent and Trademark Office.

The trademark Dell® is reigstered in the U.S. Patent and Trademark Office.

ISBN: 0-440-21096-8

RL: 6.0

Reprinted by arrangement with the author

Printed in the United States of America

November 1991

10 9 8 7 6 5 4 3 2 1

RAD

This one is for
Roberta,
with love from Dad

Contents

· · · · · · · · · · ·

The Place
· · · · · · · · · ·

THAT WAS THE DAY Sweet Mary from Boston almost burned down The Place, not once but twice. The day it all started, I mean, and how I got the money.

Sweet Mary was a chain smoker. She was seventy years old if she was a day but she insisted she was only fifty-eight, and she wore rouge, powder and thick orange lipstick, even when she was sick and coughing and couldn't get out of bed. She smoked all the time (it was against the rules to smoke in the rooms: you could only smoke in the recreation lounge downstairs) and she smoked those cigarettes with the filters in the flip-top box like the geezers sell on the television. She'd light one cigarette from another and finally fall asleep.

That's what happened that afternoon. She fell asleep in her bed and the smoke came pouring out of the ward, and Harold Hennifer, who was in charge for the moment because Mr. Jones, the superintendent, was downtown doing the weekly shopping, came running down the hall yelling and screaming "Fire, fire," his thin neck giving him the look of a chicken scrambling from an ax. The fireman arrived with the sirens wailing, and a crowd gathered outside even though The Place is out in the country. The motorcycle boys came thundering up the highway, and old Pete Honiker cackled and laughed and trembled with excitement when usually he just sits there all day long, not saying a word.

They carried Sweet Mary out of the ward, two firemen, and she looked like a queen, waving to us as if she'd done something proud and wonderful, and you could see how happy she was even though her face was all red and her eyes watery and her rouge streaked, because she always liked people to pay attention to her. Harold scurried along behind, scolding and fretting, but Sweet Mary ignored him and kept waving and smiling at us. They moved her into a room by herself because she was sick, anyway. She had a terrible cough that you could hear all over The Place at night.

All of us went in to see her. It was against the rules for the men to enter the women's section but Harold was so upset he didn't notice. He stood at the foot of the bed, telling Mary that if she was caught smoking again anywhere in the infirmary they'd send her away, maybe to the reformatory, and she started crying and looked at me and said: "Can they do that, Tommy? Can they send me to jail?"

I said to Harold: "Is this all you've got to do, go around making people cry?"

Maybe it wasn't fair to say that to him because Harold was very nervous to begin with and his face was raw with pimples and that day he had a new pimple near his nose, and it looked sore and fiery. He was the assistant superintendent, or at least that's what they called him, but he was more like one of us, an inmate. (Mr. Jones hated that word and referred to us as "guests.") Harold was not thirty years old yet but he had this trouble none of us could understand and sometimes he'd burst out crying over nothing at all.

"You old people always stick together, even if it means burning down the place," he said. "Suppose she got burned to death?"

"I wouldn't be that lucky," Sweet Mary said, and she started coughing. She always had an answer, Sweet Mary.

Finally, the excitement died down and the firemen went away and Harold opened all the windows in the ward although it hadn't been much of a fire, just the blankets scorched. The crowd outside left, straggling away slow and easy the way people do after a fire, kind of disappointed that it wasn't a real big one. Even the motorcycle boys rode off with their motors roaring softer than usual.

Stretch and I went down to the recreation lounge where the television set was and looked at the cartoons that come on just before suppertime. I thought of Sweet Mary up there in the room without any cigarettes and I was dying for one myself but, I don't know, I just couldn't make myself light up.

I got tired of the cartoons, that Popeye, and I only looked at them mostly to hear the music. They always play songs that were popular a long time ago and they sound old-fashioned and tinny, and sometimes I just closed my eyes and listened, ignoring Popeye and Olive Oyl and the others. But I got tired of even the music that day and went over and looked out the window. It was spring, almost Memorial Day, and the grass was deep green because there'd been a lot of rain that week. The sun was hidden behind clouds low and dark near the hills in the distance and the hills were smoky and alone, the way they look on rainy days. I saw Annabel Lee near the garage, pushing her face into a cluster of lilac, her long hair glistening from the dampness like dew on the grass, and I thought how nice she looked and how things would be all right if only everyone could see her like that, from a distance, a cloud of lilac at her face.

The bell rang for supper. I didn't feel like eating but the

others got up and began to leave, lingering near the door for a last look at the crazy cartoon. I stayed behind and so did Stretch. After a while we were alone, and he came and stood beside me and both of us were just there, looking out, and the television going, and nobody looking at it.

Stretch had a long, sad face and his cheeks were peppered with freckles that weren't freckles any longer but sort of brown splotches. Sometimes I'd get angry with him because he looked so mournful, and I would stay away from him. I'd get angry because I try to be cheerful and optimistic and even collect old jokes and write them down in my little black book, believing that a man should look on the bright side of things. But people come along like Stretch and Sweet Mary and old Knobby the handyman and I get to feeling that I've got to keep them cheered up and sometimes I don't feel like cheering anybody up.

Early darkness was beginning to spread outside the window and you could almost see the dandelions folding up like they do in the evening. The hills were fading in the distance, gathered up in the dusk. I never used to pay attention to hills or trees or flowers because there were so many other things to keep a man busy: my job downtown and all my friends, pretty girls to look at, and the hustle and bustle. But I found out that the hills and the sky and the grass stay around long after other things have gone. I felt like mentioning that to Stretch, how Mother Nature can be a friend, but I figured he would only find something sad to say about it and spoil the thought. Then, for some reason, he got into one of his talkative moods and started telling me again about the time he lost the letter from Babe Ruth.

I'd heard the story a hundred times and I often got restless while he told it but at least there were some happy parts in the story and it was good to see him enjoying himself. Anyway, Stretch used to pitch in the semiprofessional league in town years ago and I guess he must have been a good ballplayer. He didn't brag but there was pride in his voice when he talked about the game and those old days. And he was proudest of all of that letter from Babe Ruth.

"I made a lot of money with that letter," he said, shaking his head, remembering, as we stood at the window. "I'd be in a bar and everybody would be talking baseball and I'd say, kind of in an offhand way: 'I remember the time Babe Ruth sent me that letter.' And they'd say: 'What letter, why should Babe Ruth send *you* a letter?' "

This was my favorite part because he'd chuckle and look happy for a change.

"Well," he said, "I'd just smile a little at the fellows in the bar and tell them that I had the letter, all right, in a special wallet I bought to keep it in. And then somebody'd always want to make a bet and, sure enough, I'd take that old letter out and show it off and you never saw people so surprised in all your life . . ."

He stopped talking for a minute, hitting the palm of one hand with his fist as if he was standing out there in the pitcher's box waiting for the catcher to give him a sign.

"Boy, I sure made a lot of money with that letter and got set up with free beer," he said. Then his face got all sad again, long as January, and I knew the sorrowful part was coming. "It was sure a bad day when I lost it . . ."

"You lost it?" I asked. He always waited for me to ask him that question.

"Yep, I lost my letter when I lost my wallet and nobody ever found it. Or they never brought it back, anyways. I even put an ad in the paper. *Lost, one brown leather wallet on*

Main Street near the police station. Valuable letter inside. Keep wallet and also collect reward but return letter. I sat up half the night putting that ad together, doping it out at the kitchen table. But nobody brought it back, not even for the reward. . . ."

He was quiet a long time then, thinking about that letter, I guess, and I was thinking, too, about all the things you lose.

"The letter said . . . do you want to hear what the letter said, Tommy?" he asked suddenly.

"Sure," I told him, glad to see him eager again.

"The letter said: *Dear Stretch, No, I do not use black molasses in the winter. Thanks for the thought. Signed, Babe Ruth.* I wrote to ask him if he used black molasses in the winter because I heard that eating it was bad for your muscles and telling him he'd better stop if he did. Can you imagine him answering that letter, Tommy?" Still full of the wonder of it all, he scratched at his sagging cheek. "Why, I'd show that letter in the saloons and everybody was surprised and wanted to know all about it and one time we even called up a newspaper office and talked to some reporter who had an autograph of Babe Ruth on a scoreboard and he came down and the signatures matched and then everybody stood me to a drink." He closed his eyes and said: "*Dear Stretch, No, I do not use black molasses in the winter. Thanks for the thought. Signed, Babe Ruth.* And then I lost it . . ."

His voice was so mournful that I began to get irritated, thinking of all the sad stories in the world and how there was nothing you could do but listen. People never tell you things you can help them with. How could anybody get his letter back, much less me? I told myself that there probably wasn't any letter at all, maybe it was just something he'd made up and got to believing after a while. I felt better and not so sad about the letter but I felt worse, too, at the same time.

Suddenly, there was all this yelling from upstairs and feet running down the halls and somebody yelled: "Fire." Stretch and I started out of the lounge and I prayed that Sweet Mary hadn't started this one.

But she had, all right.

They wouldn't let us in the women's section this time because Mr. Jones was back. The firemen didn't even come and Pete Honiker pouted as he stood in the window listening for the sirens that never sounded. Mr. Jones used an extinguisher to douse the fire in Sweet Mary's blankets, or at least that's the story we heard as we stood in the hallway beyond the big heavy door that separated the men's quarters from the women's.

Knobby kept bringing us reports about what was happening. He was an old Negro who did odd jobs around The Place. Mr. Jones let him go anywhere in the infirmary as long as he took his bucket and mop or a dust rag along and kept working. Anyway, Knobby kept running out and telling us the story in little pieces like a movie serial. He told us how Sweet Mary fell asleep again with a cigarette going full steam in her mouth and how the lighted tip fell on the blanket and how Mr. Jones was sweating all over the place. Mr. Jones perspired a lot and we used to get a kick out of seeing him wiping away at his forehead on the coldest day of the year, or trying to keep his arms pressed close to his body during the summer so that we wouldn't see the sweat stains on his shirt at the armpits. But none of us chuckled or said anything that day when Knobby told us about the sweating. Then Knobby ran out again and said that Sweet Mary was crying with pain because she'd torn her lip when she pulled the cigarette out of her mouth after the smoke awakened her.

We were all quiet in the hallway because we knew that the fire meant doom for Sweet Mary. There were two things that the people at The Place feared: being taken away to the reformatory if they got into trouble or being sent to the hospital if they got sick. I looked at the fellows standing there with me. There was Stretch who was probably thinking about his lost letter or his dead wife, Lou; the old Pete Honiker all pulled into himself and shivering once in a while; and Awful Arthur, the young drunkard, his face unshaved and the thirst burning in his eyes; and fat Harry Herman who figured out forty years ago that nobody would be allowed to starve in the United States of America and swore that he'd never work again and never did; and all the others standing around. It struck me that they weren't a bad bunch. Sometimes we got on each other's nerves but we tried to make the best of it. We were all thrown together at The Place and there was no place else to go.

Officially, The Place was the Monument City Infirmary because nobody is supposed to say "poorhouse" anymore, but everybody there was poor, not only in money but in other ways: poor in friends and poor in family and poor in jobs. The Place was a rambling old building on the outskirts of Monument, set back from the highway that leads to Worcester. The city was proud of it, in a way. Once a month, the members of the Board of Welfare used to visit and they'd bring along some city official or other. They'd point out the grass and the trees outdoors, and the clean paint on the walls and the scrubbed floors, and say how wonderful it was because these poor people kept the place up, painting and fixing. That was true: everybody had chores except a few sickly ones who would cost the city too much money in a private nursing home but weren't sick enough for a hospital, or nervous people who couldn't hold a job but weren't nervous enough to be sent to an asylum.

There was a workshop in the basement and the visitors liked to stand around and watch the people as they sandpapered an old table or made a lamp out of a jug, and they'd ask questions, slow and careful. They always acted surprised when you answered them, as if they were visiting a zoo and suddenly one of the animals talked. I usually took a walk out into the fields when the visitors came, slamming the door behind me.

Mr. Jones got annoyed when I took a walk because he liked me to guide the visitors around.

"I'm sorry, Mr. Jones, but you better get somebody else," I'd say. And I *was* sorry because I hated to let him down. Mr. Jones' face reminded me of a cobweb because he had so many lines streaking every which way and he was round-shouldered as if some terrible load was piled on his back. He always used this terrible deodorant to cover the smell of his sweating. Sometimes when I saw him heading in my direction, I used to avoid him because a man can stand just so much sadness. His wife and three children had been killed in a train crash a few years ago and Annabel Lee was all he had left in the world. She was almost fourteen now and her body was still growing, but the accident had stopped her mind from developing and in many ways she would always be eight years old. She lived at The Place with us because Mr. Jones couldn't bear the thought of sending her away to an institution, and every day he drove her downtown to some special classes at one of the schools. Anyway, I'd see him coming down the hall and I'd think of that moment when they told him that his wife and three small children were dead, all of them at once, and sometimes I couldn't make myself look at him.

That day as I stood with the others near the big dark oak door that separated us from the women's section I was thinking of what a sad bunch we were and that even Mr. Jones was trapped like the rest of us.

"Well, I guess Sweet Mary's going to be sent away," Stretch said, mournful as usual.

"No use looking on the dark side of the street," I said.

"Yes, sir, Sweet Mary's going to beat you out of this place, in spite of all your talk about leaving, Tommy," Harry Herman said. "I guess everybody's going to beat you out of this place . . ."

"Don't you worry about me, Hungry Harry," I said. "I'm going, any day now . . ." I called him Hungry Harry because he had the biggest appetite of any man who didn't believe in working.

He chuckled at his joke with me but he meant no offense. Harry liked everybody and always walked around pleased with himself, figuring he had outtricked the whole world.

Awful Arthur asked Knobby: "Where'n hell she get the cigarette? I thought Mr. Jones cut her off . . ." Arthur had been cut off from liquor so many times that he was interested in things like that.

Knobby shook his head in admiration. "You know Sweet Mary. She got the loan of a cigarette from one of the firemen what was here this afternoon . . ."

"There's no flies on Sweet Mary," Stretch said.

But nobody laughed or smiled or said anything, because we knew that her days at The Place were over.

MR. JONES came into my room after the lights were out that night. Most of the men lived in the wards, but a man was allowed a room of his own if he kept it neat and clean and behaved himself. I lived alone because I like crowds fine out in the street but not in a bedroom, and besides, the wards have a smell about them, an odor of something old and passed by, that paint or soap and water never can erase.

My room had a barber's chair in the middle of it, nailed to the floor, one of those old-fashioned leather kind with the headrest and everything, and it swiveled around. My room had been the barbershop in the old days, the days when the place was filled up, a *real* poorhouse, before the government started handing out pensions and all kinds of checks. Knobby liked to come into the room and sit in the barber's chair and send himself spinning until he got dizzy. He kept it oiled and shined.

Sometimes Stretch couldn't sleep at night. His wife had been dead for fifteen years but for some reason he'd started to think about her again, especially at night, and he'd come into my room and sit in the barber's chair. In my sleep, I would feel somebody nearby and I'd wake up and see him there and we'd sit the rest of the night out together, not saying much, just waiting for dawn to come. I didn't mind because I don't need much sleep anyway, and the older I get the longer I can go without sleeping.

Anyway, Mr. Jones came into my room, slamming the door in anger and mopping his forehead. "We've got to send Mary to the hospital," he said.

"Too bad," I answered.

"Look, Tommy," he said, scowling, the cobweb lines tightening up, "don't act like I'm a criminal or something. And it's not because of the fires she started, although we can't take the risk of having her burn down the place. The doctor came up a couple of hours ago and says she's got double pneumonia. Mary can never do anything by halves—she'd got to get *double* pneumonia."

He gave the barber chair a spin. "Mary asked me a special favor. Why she rates special favors I'll never know, but anyway, she wants to see you. Alone." He covered his mouth and belched.

"Take it easy, Mr. Jones," I said. "You'll get indigestion." I kept my voice gentle because it was one of those times when I could almost see the ghosts of his dead wife and children standing near him.

"It's against the rules," he said. "You know I can't let a man and woman alone in a room in this place, Tommy." He went to the window and looked out and then turned to me, sighing. "Anyway, she's so damn sick that I told her you could go up for ten minutes. Tonight—because there'll be too many people around in the morning." A drop of perspiration rolled down his nose. "Between Harold not knowing how to run things and me breaking the rules and fires starting all over the place, I'm going to lose my job someday . . ."

"You're a good man, Mr. Jones," I said.

"That won't help when the Board asks me to resign," he

said, scowling again. "Now remember, Tommy. Ten minutes. And for God's sake, don't give her a cigarette . . ."

There was no doubt that Sweet Mary was sick. She was sitting up in bed, supported by two pillows, and her chin and jowls sagged loosely. Her lipstick and rouge stood out sharply against her pale skin as if some children had been daubing at her like they do with faces on billboards.

"Tommy, they're going to send me away," she wailed as Mr. Jones left us alone in the room, careful to swing the door wide open as he went out.

"Maybe the hospital will fix you up and put you on your feet again, Sweet Mary," I said, trying to make my voice cheerful.

"I've got a feeling I'll never get better," she said, coughing up and spitting into a twisted piece of Kleenex. The coughing stopped and she looked up at me. "How come you always call me Sweet Mary from Boston?" she asked. Old people are like that, always changing the subject.

"I don't know. I always give everybody names of my own, according to what they are. Like Awful Arthur and Hungry Harry. Maybe because you look kind of sweet, like one of those aristocrats from Boston . . ."

She was alone and sick and it didn't cost anything to say that. The reason I started calling her Sweet Mary from Boston was because she didn't look sweet at all with her painted face and her tired hair that had been dyed too many times. I added the Boston part because I always smiled thinking how Mary would shock those proper dowagers on Beacon Hill that I've read about in the newspapers.

"I'm glad you always thought I was sweet," she said. She looked shy suddenly. "You know I had seven children, Tommy?"

I'd never thought of her as a wife or a mother or a grand-mother even, or that she must have been young once and pretty, and maybe sweet, after all.

"Yes, seven children, all grown up now and lots of grand-children by this time, I guess," she said. She started to cry again and she was a messy crier, coughing and struggling and sobbing. "I need a cigarette," she said, "goodness, I need a cigarette."

"You'll get us both thrown out of here," I said. I half closed the door and returned and gave her a cigarette. "Now, smoke fast," I said, worried and impatient.

"Maybe I wasn't the best woman in the world," she said, "but when the kids were young I was all right, a good mother. No running around and I didn't touch a drop. Then Sam died, he was my husband, and everything went to pot. But at least I saw the kids grow up and my youngest is some kind of a professor now, a real professor in a fancy college out in the Midwest . . ." She was smoking away like a steam engine and I was getting real nervous, afraid that Mr. Jones might suddenly walk in.

"Mary, why don't you let me get in touch with one of your kids?" I asked. "I could telephone from down-stairs . . ."

She shook her head violently and started to cough again, beads of sweat standing out on her forehead like raindrops. She handed me the cigarette, and I went to the window and slipped it out.

"They don't want to see me now," she said. "I disgraced them all too much before I left and I think they were glad to see me go." The coughing stopped and she breathed easier. "Anyway, they probably think I'm already dead."

I always told people to have children, to raise big families, to surround themselves with kids so that they would have plenty of love around them through the years and some comfort in their old age. But I looked at Sweet Mary on the bed, her kids grown up and not knowing where she was and not caring enough to find out, and I thought: I'll never tell that to anybody again.

"Tommy," she said, beckoning me closer and raising herself a little. "Go to my pocketbook there on the bureau and bring it to me . . ."

Her pocketbook was a yellow straw handbag decorated with red and white artificial flowers that were battered and faded. She pulled out a solid white envelope that had an elastic band around it.

"There's sixty-three dollars in there, Tommy," she said, putting the envelope in my hand. "I kept it hidden all the time I've been here and, believe me, it was no joke trying to hide it the way they kept searching me for cigarettes."

"You mean you have sixty-three dollars and you've been living here all the time?"

She shrugged wearily. "It's not enough money to support anybody, not enough to live on, Tommy. Only enough to think on. That's what kept my spirits up when I'd get the blues. I'd say to myself: Some weekend I'm going to take my sixty-three dollars and get me a room in a real hotel and call room service. You don't know how many fine hotels I've been in, laying here in this place at night with my eyes closed." She put her hand on mine and it was soft and warm and moist. "I want you to have that money, Tommy. It's yours, all of it. You've been the only person nice to me in a long time, always cheering me up and sneaking me cigarettes and calling me sweet when I'm not sweet. Nobody ever called me sweet before, not even when I was young and kind of sweet, if I do say so myself . . ."

I told her that I couldn't take her money, that I couldn't do a thing like that.

"Look, Tommy, I'm old and sick and they're taking me to the hospital and I know I'll never leave the hospital, never. You get so you can feel those things."

I tried to give her back the envelope but she said, "For a long time you've been talking about leaving here and going downtown and getting started again. But you never had the means. Well, that sixty-three dollars ought to be enough to start you off, anyway."

I began to argue with her but we heard the sound of footsteps. "Hide the money, Tommy, hide it," she urged. "If Mr. Jones finds it, he's got to turn it over to the Board."

I shoved the envelope in my pants pocket as Mr. Jones entered. He looked suspicious as he pushed the door open all the way and began to sniff the air.

Sweet Mary burst out crying when she saw him.

"For God's sake," he cried, his patience at an end, I guess, but she kept right on bawling.

Mr. Jones took out his handkerchief. It was damp and limp as usual but he wiped his face with it. He shook his head in disgust and took my arm and hurried me toward the door. I held him off a second and called to her before Mr. Jones pushed me into the hall: "Take care of yourself, Sweet Mary." But I don't think she heard me, she was coughing and crying so much.

I went back to my room and put her envelope in the bottom of my drawer under the clothes. I stood there thinking about her until Knobby came in and sat in the barber's chair even though he wasn't supposed to be roaming around at that time of night. He always sat gingerly in the chair, glancing toward the door now and then because he was afraid that Stretch would come in and find him there. For some reason, Stretch didn't like to see Knobby enjoying himself in the chair. See how people get? They have these quirks about them and I have my funny ways, too, but you've got to let old people act like that. It lets them be persons.

Knobby liked to have me read him jokes from my little black book, but I didn't feel in the mood just then. He'd heard them all a thousand times anyway. But he sat there with those black eyes of his so full of some kind of lonesomeness that I finally read him a few jokes.

He listened closely, like a little kid hearing a bedtime story, nodding his head, although he didn't laugh at all: he never laughed at the jokes although he liked to hear them.

I got tired of reading and stopped, and he said: "Read me some of them ladies-gentlemen poems, Tommy."

I was famous in The Place for those poems. Some I had made up myself but I never admitted it because I didn't want anybody to think I was a poet; poets are supposed to be eccentric.

"All right," I said, because to tell the truth I always enjoyed reciting those poems. I started out with:

> "Ladies and gentlemen,
>   Why is it I cry?
>   I went around all day
>   With an unbuttoned fly . . ."

That's one I made up and everybody thinks it's funny. Knobby didn't laugh, of course, just listened quietly. I think he really believed it was serious poetry like you find in books.

I read him a few more and his head started to droop and I dropped my voice to a whisper. I read the words automatically because I kept thinking of Sweet Mary. I made up my mind to keep her money safe and take it to her in the hospital.

After a while, Knobby fell asleep in the barber's chair and I went to bed but I hardly slept at all.

EVERY SATURDAY MORNING in fair weather Annabel Lee and I would sit out on the park bench that Mr. Jones got from the city when it became too old for the Common downtown. The bench, which Stretch had painted blazing red, stood out under the weeping-willow tree on the back lawn and on Saturday mornings Annabel Lee would sit with me and work at her drawing for the "Good Friend Page."

Her name was Annie but I often called her Annabel Lee. It was a name I saw in a poem that I read once in night school. The poem was sad, about a girl who was still a child and lived in a lonely kingdom by the sea, and when I first saw Annie the name leaped at me across the years.

The "Good Friend Page" was something the newspaper printed every Saturday morning, a half-page really, filled with jokes and puzzles and games for children. There was one special feature, "Jigsaw Lines," where the newspaper printed a couple of lines that didn't make any sense and the kids were supposed to use them to make a drawing. The best drawing of all would be printed the following week and the winner was sent a fancy certificate. That was Annabel Lee's big ambition, to have her drawing appear in the paper. Every Saturday she struggled to make something out of those lines, but she didn't have much control over her fingers and most of the time you couldn't recognize what she had drawn. Once I tried to help her but she looked at me in disappointment, and reminded me that I myself had told her nobody could help, according to the rules. A lot of things she forgot, but she remembered sometimes.

She brought me the paper that Saturday, frowning as she searched the page for the picture of her drawing. Then she looked up at me bright-eyed, not discouraged at all. "This week I'll show them, Tommy, I'll show them," she said, hopeful and eager. But she glanced at the paper again, her face wistful.

I felt sorry because there was nothing I could do to help her. A while back I'd even thought of writing to that newspaper and asking them to print her drawing as a special favor because of her condition but I never did. You never do the fine, shining things that you should. I figured, anyway, that Mr. Jones would be embarrassed, if he knew I'd written to the newspaper. He liked to go along pretending that Annie was as normal as any girl.

Birds were scattering in the trees and dew was still sparkling on the grass and the wind rose a little. I didn't like to watch Annabel Lee struggling with the pencil so I looked out toward the front of The Place where I could see a part of the road and thought what a fine day it would be to go downtown and get my old job back and stand on my own two feet again. Some days I didn't feel like going anywhere and other days it was all I could do to sit still and not fill up my suitcase and call a taxi.

"Is Sweet Mary coming back?" Annie asked me, putting down her pencil and blowing air out of the side of her mouth. Trying to draw always tired her out.

"Maybe," I said. "When she gets better . . ."

"She told me one time she has lots of children some-where," she said.

"Far away from here, too far," I answered.

"Do you have some children, too, somewhere, Tommy?"

"No," I said. You couldn't give her long answers because she would begin to frown, lost in so many words.

"Did you ever have children?"

"No," I said, again. There was the baby, of course, but I didn't want to explain it all to her. The baby lived only twenty-one minutes (the nurse told me the time exactly), twenty-one minutes, and I didn't even have a name to give him because Sophie had set her mind on a girl. Carol, she was going to call the baby, if it was a girl.

"Don't you have nobody?" she asked. "Nobody at all, Tommy?"

"No," I said, sad for a moment and then sorry for being sad in front of her.

"I'm lucky I've got Daddy," she said.

"Yes, you're lucky, Annabel Lee."

"Did you have a daddy one time?"

She was a great one for questions. Once she got started she could go on all day and it was like playing ping-pong with words, tossing them back and forth between us.

"Oh, yes," I answered. "I had a daddy and a mother and even brothers and sisters. Five brothers and two sisters, and we all lived in a big tenement once, the kind you see down-town . . ."

"And what happened to them, Tommy? Did they all go away?"

"Yes, Annie," I said. "They all went away . . ."

"If my daddy went away, you're the daddy I'd like to have," she said.

"Thank you, Annie."

"What are you sad about, Tommy? You look so sad, like the weeping willow . . ."

"I'm not sad, Annie. Just that my eyes get tired blinking in the sun and that makes me look sad." I thought I should tell her a funny story like I do sometimes but I couldn't think of anything funny.

We sat there quietly and she went back to her drawing, and I could see she was doing a terrible job as usual, the lines squirming this way and that on the page. But she worked with patience, her little tongue in the corner of her lips and her teeth biting down on it and the soft hair tumbling over one cheek. So many times she looked pretty.

"Why is it you never go downtown, Tommy?" she asked, starting again, putting down the pencil.

"Oh, I go downtown every Sunday to church," I said.

"I mean, go downtown like everybody else," she said. "Mr. Herman says you'll never go back downtown. He says a man"—She paused, trying to pin down his exact words—"a man of advanced years has no business running around down there." She frowned. "Are you a man of advanced years, Tommy?"

"Do I look like one?" I asked, rankled at Hungry Harry who always twits people about age just because he's only sixty-six.

Annabel Lee studied my face for a while.

"Yes," she said.

She didn't know how to lie to make somebody feel good.

"Listen," I said, changing the subject, "I'm going back downtown someday. I'm saving up and I'm going. And not only for a visit."

"Are you going to leave and never come back?" she asked,

her face clouding up. I felt sad and good at the same time: sad to see *her* feeling sad, and good to know that she wouldn't want me to go.

I touched her hair. The softness of it was gentle on my fingertips.

"Oh, not for a long time yet," I said.

"How long?" she asked, sitting there with her hands in her lap, patient, concentrating on her questions and answers.

"So long you don't have to worry about it," I said.

Satisfied at last, she sighed and went back to her work. After a while, she held it up for me to see. I couldn't recognize a thing on the paper.

"Why, that's fine, Annie," I said.

She beamed. "I like it better when you call me Annabel Lee," she said. "I like that. The other day one of the cycle boys asked me my name and I said: 'Annabel Lee.' And he said: 'Like in the poem they have in school?' And I said: 'Yes.' And I was proud he knew my name from a poem, Tommy . . ."

"You shouldn't talk to those motorcycle boys," I said.

There was an old water pump that didn't work anymore across the street from The Place and the motorcycle boys used it as a spot to gather at and to organize their formations. They'd ride up the highway on those big roaring motorcycles, wearing those black, shiny jackets with the brass hobnails on them.

"Why shouldn't I talk to them?" she asked. "I love those cycles. *Whee* they go, *whee* . . . and all that noise. Like they could take you to the moon . . ."

I thought of how little innocence there was left in the world and so much of it there beside me.

"Why shouldn't I talk to them?" she asked again, in that quiet patient way.

"Oh, they're not the right kind of boys. They're a lot bigger and older and kind of wild . . ."

"Animals are wild," she said. "Are they like animals, you mean?"

She thought that every word had only one meaning and often took the wrong meaning, so you had to watch yourself with her.

"Not animals," I said. "Just kind of fast moving. I didn't mean wild like animals." But sometimes I wondered. We'd sit on the veranda during the day or in the evening and see them coming, those motorcycles, kicking up the dust, and throbbing by, and it seemed they always turned up their motors near The Place, racing them and making them roar, upsetting the ladies. One time we saw them surround a car that was being driven by a woman all alone. The boys drew their motorcycles up around her car, at the sides and in the front and back, and she passed our place looking helpless and frightened. Mr. Jones complained to the police a few times about the noise, especially at night in the summer when we'd hear them racing by, but the police said the boys weren't committing any crime. The police said they were just young and full of juices and had a club that promoted safety on the highways and it was better to have them out on the road, anyway, where everybody could see them, than have them becoming juvenile delinquents, hanging around back alleys or the barrooms.

She didn't say anything for a while, just sat hugging herself with her arms. "Annabel Lee," she said in a dreaming way, her voice soft. She giggled, leaning toward me, and whispered: "One of those boys asked me if I wanted a ride on the cycle. He has a nice seat on the back." She paused, thinking hard. "Sheepskin, he said, nice and soft, and he said we'd go sailing over the road." She looked up and saw my face. "What's the matter, Tommy?"

I was seeing her in a different way from ever before, not as little Annabel Lee who never grew up beyond eight years old but as a girl turning fourteen, becoming a woman almost, with soft places about her and a kind of loveliness when she turned her head just so, and if you didn't look straight at her and didn't see the right eye that was off center a bit, or the funny twist to the side of her mouth.

"Nothing's the matter," I said, "but I think it's best if you stay away from those boys. When you see them pull up across the road, you better stay here at The Place . . ."

"I'd like to ride on a cycle," she said, "sitting on a sheepskin seat . . ."

A chill went through me. I remembered hearing what happened when Mr. Jones first sent her to the regular school downtown, before he admitted to himself that there was something wrong with her. The kids would poke fun at her and send her off on foolish errands. Stretch said that they would tell her crazy stories that made her wake up screaming at night but she would come home every day happy that everybody was paying attention to her, bursting with joy about the wonderful things that had happened. She'd tell how the kids had let her play tag and how she was the lucky one because she was "it" all the time, and how they sent her across the street to the store at recess time to ask the man there for an ExLax lollipop. And Mr. Jones saw finally how it was and he enrolled her in the special classes.

"It's better to ride in a car," I said, "the way you do when your daddy takes you downtown . . ."

She didn't hear me, I guess. "The wind tosses your hair," she said, "that's what the boy told me, the wind tosses your hair, and you can go sixty an hour. Is that fast, Tommy, sixty an hour?"

"Too fast," I said. "You could fall off and hurt yourself. And think how your daddy would feel . . ." I wondered whether I should tell Mr. Jones about the motorcycles and yet I didn't want to upset him. The city didn't like the idea of Annie living at The Place with a bunch of old people, some of them nervous and strange and some of them unstable like Awful Arthur. Mr. Jones had had to do some fast talking with the Board to let her stay, promising there'd be no trouble. He had a separate apartment in The Place where he and Annie lived and he tried to watch her carefully all the time.

She still wasn't listening to me. "The boy had a brush, like the brush daddy uses to brush his clothes, and he brushed the seat and said: 'Come along, Annabel Lee, how about a ride?' And then another boy said: 'Come on, lay off, Rudy, can't you see what she is?' " She paused, thinking hard. "I didn't like that boy. What did he mean, Tommy—see what she is?"

She could take you by surprise at times. "He meant you're a young girl, that's all," I answered. "And young girls shouldn't be riding on motorcycles . . ."

"The silver palace, to the silver palace," she said, half singing the words. She had no sense of pitch at all, but she loved music and Mr. Jones bought her phonograph records all the time, those kiddie records with fairy tales being sung on them. "Do you think there are silver palaces in the world, Tommy?" she asked.

"There's a lot of places in the world," I said, thinking that it was just as well she believed in those fairy tales.

She held up her drawing. "You going to sign it, Tommy?"

I took her pencil and wrote on the back as I did every week:

"This work is original by Miss Ann Jones, age 13$\frac{1}{2}$, and she did not have any help. Signed, Thomas Bartin."

The rules said that you had to write that on the back of the drawing. I looked at the picture again, hoping to see some figure there to recognize, and it did look a little like a teakettle. She didn't offer to say what it was and I dared not ask her because then she'd have known the drawing wasn't good enough to win a certificate.

"I really would like to ride on one of those cycles," she said, her bad eye going way off center, the way it did when she got tired.

That night, I heard the roaring of the motorcycles in my sleep all night long.

Sᴜɴᴅᴀʏ ᴡᴀs ᴛʜᴇ ʙᴇsᴛ and the worst day at The Place. It was going to church and Open House and dressing up and no chores but a lot of other things, too.

The best part was morning. Mr. Jones always drove Minnie and me down to the half-past-five Mass at St. Jude's Church and dropped us off while he ate breakfast at the Mechanic Street Diner. The reason he did this was because Minnie was the cook at the infirmary and she liked to get the Mass over with so she could concentrate on the big dinner of the week, fried chicken. He took me along because he always left me in charge of The Place later, while he drove back and forth from town, taking the other people to the different Masses at the two Catholic churches and to the services at the Protestant churches. It was nice being in charge of The Place, strolling around like a foreman and answering the telephone, although the telephone didn't ring often and there was not much to do. But it makes a man feel good to have some responsibility.

I like going to church, that early Mass, because it cheers a man's spirit to see the priest at the altar, pure and holy, and to smell the wax from the burning candles and see the people bowed in prayer. It gives you a feeling that somebody cares about the things worth caring about. When my mother was living, she'd get all upset if she heard me come in the house late at night and flop into bed without kneeling to say my prayers. But I slacked off praying after she died. I mean, there are so many people to pray for. I used to pray for the souls of Sophie and my mother and father and all my relatives who are dead and the old friends who passed away; and the living people, too, people I used to work with or somebody in trouble. But once you get started praying for everybody there's no end to it. Anyway, I used to kneel down and pray for everybody, and the list got so long that sometimes I fell asleep on my knees. Then I went the other way and didn't pray at all. The reason I stopped was that I'd started praying for myself, especially after Sophie died. And all the while I prayed for myself I felt guilty, thinking of all the people in the world who *really* needed help from God, and to tell the truth, I got so confused after a while that I finally settled for the old prayers I learned when I was a boy, the ones my mother taught me: the *Notre Père* and *Je Vous Salue, Márie,* and the *Confiteor* and *Acte de Contrition.* Sometimes I left off the *Confiteor* because it's pretty long.

Anyway, Mr. Jones would bring Minnie and me back to The Place and she would be in charge of the kitchen and I would be the boss of the rest of the infirmary because Minnie never liked anyone hanging around while she was working.

Minnie was a short, round woman with a motherly bosom and gray hair. She always reminded me of Joe Palooka's mother in the funny papers. One time she baked me a special cake for some reason or other and I was so touched by the gesture that I wanted to pay her a compliment and I said: "You know something, Minnie? You look just like Joe Palooka's mother in the funny papers."

It was like you see in the movies: she picked up a frying

pan and threw it at me. "Listen, Tommy Bartin," she said, after the pan had bounced off the wall, denting the plaster, "I don't want any sassy stuff from you or anybody else . . ."

It didn't do any good to tell her that I *liked* Joe Palooka's mother. I mean, how could anybody help liking Joe Palooka's nice old fat mother? But I kept out of Minnie's way and she never baked me another cake and it made me feel bad, that whole situation, because the only nice thing you can do for people, if you haven't any money, is to pay them a compliment once in a while. And it reminded me a little bit of all the people downtown who become suspicious if you try to do something nice for them.

Anyway, the emptiest part of the day was the afternoon during the visiting hours. A city infirmary isn't like a hospital or nursing home because if you had anybody that cared enough you wouldn't be there in the first place and the sign out front that said *Sunday Open House 2 to 5* always seemed to me like the saddest sign in the world.

The women used to pretend that someone was coming, some nephew they'd always favored or some old friend. They'd get themselves fixed up fancy and sit on the veranda in the nice weather and wait through the tired afternoon, watching the cars going by. Sweet Mary used to put on her fancy jewelry and have her hair done up just so and she'd sit and wait with the others.

After Sweet Mary was taken to the hospital, I was hoping that somebody would come and call for her on a visit and Mr. Jones would say that it was too late, that she was in the hospital. That would serve them right for making her wait all those Sundays.

The men never expected visitors and most of them never dressed up special on Sunday afternoon. That's why I was surprised when Harold poked his head into the recreation lounge and said there was a caller waiting to see me. There must be some mistake, I thought.

I went up to my room and put on my necktie, the green-and-white silk polka-dot tie Sophie bought me for our honeymoon, and I went to the front hall and there was Charlie Morrissey grinning at me, his blue eyes snapping and his bald head gleaming and the stickpin in his tie glittering.

"Tommy, Tommy," he said, shaking his head and holding out his hand as if he was going to hug me, for crying out loud.

He was a short man, and everything about him was short: he kept his fingernails pared close and wore small-boy ties because men's ties would dangle below his belt, and he liked his pants short because he had a weakness for bright, gay socks and wanted to show them off. He was such a neat man that you could hate him for it. He couldn't stand dirt and you never saw him with a sliver of lint on his suit or a streak of grime on his face even when he worked the grinding machine at the shop. He always had a crisp handkerchief peeking out of his suit-jacket pocket but he wouldn't blow his nose with it because Charlie would never think of getting a cold like other people: too messy. He was a friend from the days at the comb shop, and Charlie and Jean-Baptiste La Chapelle and I drank many a beer together at Lu's Place and sang the old songs and had good times. After a big night, Charlie would come by and try to rout me out of bed. He always looked so fresh and pink and clean that I would be disgusted with him and groan myself back to sleep.

"Good to see you, Charlie," I said, my voice too loud. "How do you like my place? It's kind of big, too many rooms, but I let a lot of friends move in and let the city pretend they own it but, what the hake, there's enough to go around . . ."

"Tommy, Tommy," he said, shaking my hand and holding on long. "Still the same Tommy. Still the same, joking and not joking at the same time. . . ." He ran his finger along the molding of the doorway in an absentminded way as if he was looking for dirt to flick away. "You still got that joke book, the black book with all the jokes in it?"

"Yep," I said. "I got the book and two pairs of shoes and two pairs of pants and my sport jacket and a good necktie and three changes of underwear and five pairs of socks. And the government gives me a check every month and I get to keep eight dollars of it after paying my room and board . . ." I shouldn't have spoken harsh that way because it was nice of him to visit me and I was really glad to see him.

Actually, Charlie was the only fellow from the old days that I ever heard from: he sent me a Christmas card every year and often jotted down some of the latest news about people and things downtown.

He looked embarrassed suddenly. "I never came here before because I figured you wouldn't want me to come," he said. "Many's the time I said to myself: Think I'll take a taxi and go visit Tommy. But I didn't think you'd want me to come and I figured that any day old Tommy'll come back to town . . ."

"Well, someday I might just do that, Charlie," I said. "When conditions are right . . ."

"Then I thought: Maybe he likes it there," Charlie went on as if I hadn't spoken at all. "And maybe by the time he gets back I'll be married already. You been here—how long, Tommy? Four, five years?"

"Charlie, I said, joshing him but serious at the same time, "don't throw away my years like that. I've been here a little over three years. Thirty-nine months . . ." Saying the years and the months out loud made them seem longer all of a sudden and I thought how funny the years get divided, all uneven: three years at The Place, and forty-five years at the shop, and ten years in school, counting night school, and a handful of years to grow up in. And out of all that time, only eighteen months with Sophie.

I was thinking of that, caught off guard for a moment because I don't like to bring back what's dead and gone, when something Charlie had said stopped me.

"Married?" I asked. "What do you mean—you might be married already?"

"I'm getting married, Tommy," he said, his eyes dancing with mischief. "That's why I came, to give you an invite to the wedding. Memorial Day, that's only three days from now. Wednesday. I'm taking the big step . . ."

He always looked happy but his happiness now was like fireworks. But at the same time I could see him watching me close and his eyes changed and there was a waiting in them. "Well, what do you think, Tommy?" he said, and I was surprised to see him acting shy, like a little boy. "Think it's kind of foolish for me to be getting hitched at my age? I'm sixty-eight . . ."

"Hake," I said, "I thought all the time you was eighty-eight . . ." And he laughed and I thought again of Sophie. It was one of those moments when I couldn't remember her face and those are the worst moments of all. But I thought of how she'd pour me a beer after work and rub her cheek against my head at the same time and I thought of all the lonesome people at The Place and Stretch missing his Lou so much. So I slapped Charlie on the shoulder and said: "You old rascal. Foolish? Why, that's the best news I heard since the day they told me you fell in a load of horse manure in your new suit . . ." I always fooled with him about his neatness.

He was all eagerness again and excited. "You really think so, Tommy? She's a wonderful woman. She's no kiddie, she's sixty-two, but a nicer woman you wouldn't want to meet. And she's a handsome one. I figure I waited this long I might's well get me a handsome one . . ."

Charlie had always praised married life, arguing that a man wasn't meant to live alone. He was married a long time ago and his wife died in the flu epidemic in the First World War and left him with two little kids to bring up.

We sat down on the bench in the hallway and he told me all about his bride-to-be. Her name was Gladys Foster and they met at a meeting of the Happy Timers Club when they played bid whist together. Whenever the club went on a picnic or maybe a bus ride to Revere Beach in Boston in the summer they'd pair off together.

"I don't know," he said, shaking his head. "I never felt comfortable with a woman, not since Aggie died. But with Gladys it's different. Why, I even gave up drinking beer for her. She hates a man to drink and the Happy Timers don't hold with drinking, anyway. And I don't miss it at all. She lives alone in a rooming house near the post office and I live up over Burton's Shoe Store because I don't want to be living with one of the kids and getting on their nerves, and it seemed like the only thing to do: get married and be together. We found this little tenement up on the west side, a little far from town but she likes it, and we've been fixing it up, painting and stuff . . ."

"Well, you've got to give the Happy Timers credit for one good thing," I said. I'd never thought much of the club, all those people banding together just because they're old. Charlie used to try to get me to go to the meetings and play cards, or go along on one of their trips to the museum in Boston or a ball game at Fenway Park, but I always stayed away from them. Just because a fellow happens to be a certain age (that was a rule of the club: you couldn't join unless you were over sixty) doesn't mean you have to be stuck with people your own age all the time.

The club has a committee that visits the sick people all over the city and once in a while four or five Happy Timers would visit The Place, and they seemed disappointed if nobody was sick. One time, one of the sick-committee members was a poor old fellow on crutches who looked like he might die before he got back to town. I was glad I was never sick when they came visiting. It would be awful to be there in bed and have a bunch of Happy Timers or somebody on crutches hobbling up to your bed to cheer you up.

"So we're getting married Memorial Day," Charlie said again, "and that's why I came up, to give you an invite. It wouldn't seem right without you there, Tommy. There's going to be a big reception in Elks Hall in the afternoon with dancing and a buffet. And the Happy Timers are giving us a party at the regular meeting the day before. Why, you could come to the party and that would be a good chance to meet them all."

"Well, we'll see, Charlie," I said, not wanting to disappoint him although I knew I wouldn't go. I didn't want to go to any wedding until I could walk in, a man with a job and some money in my pocket, not just taking a day off from a city infirmary.

He went on talking, about how he and Gladys would pool their money and their social security checks and how he had put some aside during the years. All of a sudden I wanted him to leave.

Then he seemed to run down. His face changed so that he looked worried, and I thought: What's *he* got to be worried about?

"Tommy," he said, his voice hushed. "Do you think I'm making a damn fool of myself? I didn't want to say anything about this at all, but the kids—well, they're not kids any more, all grown up with their own families and they think it's a disgrace, their old man getting married. I got six grandchildren, Tommy. Do you think it's such a disgrace?"

"Of course it's not a disgrace," I said, wanting to tell him that it was mean and shabby for his kids to feel that way but knowing that a father loves his kids even if they are mean and selfish sometimes.

"Charlie," I said, "just because a man wants a little companionship and maybe some love, too, that's nothing to be ashamed of. You marry that Happy Timers woman, Charlie. You always let those kids of yours lead their own lives, didn't you? Why, even the fancy doctors and the big experts say people should get married, no matter how old they are. Just the other day in the newspaper I was reading about that and I almost looked around for a bride myself . . ."

That wasn't true, of course, but I was trying hard to convince him.

He jumped to his feet and he was the old Charlie again, so damn neat and proper that you could have bashed him one, his sails full in the breeze and his chin tilted up. I was glad to see him happy like that but I still wished he would leave. I didn't feel like having company anymore.

"You know, Tommy," he said, "much as I wanted to come up to invite you to the wedding and the shindigs, I came to ask you about that. I mean, I know it's right and so does Gladys, she has a head on her shoulders, but I wanted to hear you say it."

He stayed awhile after that, standing at the door, making conversation about the old days at work and people there and the Happy Timers and how the old saloon we knew as Lu's Place was known now as the Golden Rooster, of all things, and after a while he called a taxi and I went with him down the walk.

"You try to make that wedding," he said.

"Charlie, I might surprise you," I told him, wishing for a minute I could go but knowing that all those old people there would depress me.

When the taxi pulled up, we shook hands and he tried to press some money into my palm but I insisted he take it back. Finally I had to shove it into the breast pocket of his jacket; it annoyed him because I rumpled his handkerchief. He got into the taxi and settled back and lighted a cigar as the car drove out of the yard, sitting there like a man going someplace.

Mr. JONES had to scold old Pete Honiker now and then because Pete broke every rule at The Place. He didn't like to take a bath like everybody else because he claimed he'd catch cold and he said he washed himself all over every night anyway, scrubbing his elbows and armpits and all the sweaty places. They'd try to get him into the bathtub on Saturday nights, calling his name down the hallways, but he'd hide someplace, in the kitchen closet or under the dining-room table or in the old, unused coalbin in the cellar. Sometimes I let him hide under my bed because I figured a man has to take a stand somewhere.

We were sitting in the recreation lounge the next afternoon and Awful Arthur started to tease Pete about the baths. Arthur teased in a mean way, nothing funny about it. There were no programs worth watching on the television, no baseball games or anything, only those serial shows drenched in organ music that the women went crazy about. I was glad they had their own television in the women's lounge.

Anyway, Awful Arthur started in on old Pete Honiker. Arthur was about forty years old, one of those geezers that you had to work pretty hard to like because he had a sharp tongue and he never had worked steady, managing to get the money for his drunken sprees by doing odd jobs around the barrooms downtown. He was a big fellow with a beer belly pushed up into his chest, giving him the shape of a milk bottle. But his arms were thin as kindling wood. He was always restless, pacing the floor, itching for a drink, and he made all of us nervous, even Mr. Jones.

Old Pete didn't answer Arthur's taunts, just shriveled up in his chair as if he was battling a cold wind, so Arthur started in on me. First he began to call me "professor" in his insulting voice.

"If you're so smart, professor, and always writing things down in books, how come you're stuck here like the rest of us?" he asked.

Most of the time I didn't pay any attention to him because it was the agony of the thirst that did it.

"They say you went to night school, professor, and had a good job at the big Frenchman's shop. A timekeeper you was, with a white shirt on. How come you end up here?"

"He got sick, that's why," Stretch answered. "He got the gallstones and had an operation and couldn't work no more . . ."

"The Frenchman didn't *want* him no more," Awful Arthur said. "That's all there was to it . . ."

"Listen, he can have his job back any time he feels like it," Stretch said. "Ain't that the truth, Tommy?"

It was nice having Stretch stick up for me but I didn't want him getting into trouble with the geezer and I figured I'd better do my own arguing.

"Arthur," I said, "I worked in that place forty-five years. I worked there when they used to bend the combs out of horn they got off the cattle from South America. And I worked there when they had the celluloid that used to flare up and start fires two or three times a week. And I worked there when they started using those fancy plastics. Now don't you think they'd always have the door open for a man like that?" I asked.

It was true: I spent most of my life in that shop the Canuck ran and I worked there when his grandfather, who started the place, would stand right at the bench working along like the others. In the good years of celluloid, when I still had all my strength and had finally gotten my diploma from the night school and Sophie would be waiting home for me when the whistle blew at five o'clock, I got promoted to timekeeper and wore a shirt and tie every day and had a yellow pencil stuck above my ear. It wasn't until the bad years after the old man died and his son Frenchy took over that the shop began to lose step with the rest of the factories in Monument. Plastics took the place of celluloid and Frenchy didn't want to invest money in the big expensive molding machines. If a shop loses step, all the people who work there lose step, too. When Frenchy finally modernized his operations, he had lost a lot of time and distance to the other shops. During my last few years there he had me sweeping the floors and doing odd jobs but I didn't mind: the important thing is to have a job, someplace to go when the sun comes up, a time card with your name on it so that you always know you're somebody, and a nice tiredness in the evening that you can lull away with a few glasses of beer. But my gallstones raised a fuss and I had that operation and later it was terrible staying up in my fourth-floor room at Miss Bein's apartment house alone all day, afraid that I wouldn't be able to climb back up the stairs if I went out. The day finally came when I asked Frenchy if I could go back to work. He had a toothache and was pacing the floor in pain and shouting that business was awful, the orders falling off and a molding machine broken down, and he said he had no place for old sick men who were only good for pushing a broom. I staggered out of the place, dizzy and weak, although I managed to slam the door behind me to show him that a man could still be independent. I headed for the nearest saloon and everybody was a stranger because everyone I knew was either dead or gone away and I wanted to stand up on a table and yell: "I'm Tommy Bartin, do you hear? I'm Tommy Bartin. I'm somebody . . ." I lurched up Mechanic Street, stopping at the bars along the way, spending my last few dollars, and later falling into a sickening darkness as the whole world began to spin away from me. I woke up the next day at The Place. Mr. Jones had brought me there after getting a call from the police: the police had found me on the Common, lying on the grass, and hadn't known whether I was sick or drunk. They always called Mr. Jones in cases like that.

But as I sat there looking at Arthur, I thought: Three years can change a lot of things and maybe Frenchy's fortunes have changed too. Maybe he's got false teeth by now (toothaches always plagued him and he hated to go to a dentist), and maybe he'll remember how I worked with his grandfather. I had a sudden feeling that if I went back to see him, and business was humming, he would hire me again. How could Frenchy turn away a man who had given forty-five years to a shop?

"Time means nothing," Awful Arthur was saying. "When a man gets to be an old duffer, experience don't mean a thing."

"Maybe I'll prove you wrong pretty soon," I said. "Maybe I'll just walk out of here someday and prove you wrong, Arthur."

He snorted. "You been talking about leaving here for a long time and you ain't gone yet, professor. You ain't ever gonna leave. You can talk fancy because you got a diploma from the night school but you ain't fooling me. The day you leave, professor, you let me know and I'll give you a thousand dollars . . ."

Pete Honiker started cackling and laughing to himself in the corner and we all looked at him because he seldom made a sound, especially when Arthur was around. Giggling, he said: "Let's see your thousand dollars, Arthur, let's see it . . ."

For some reason, that made Arthur keep quiet and he sat brooding in his chair, maybe thinking of all the booze a thousand dollars could buy. But after a while he started in on Stretch. He knew about that Babe Ruth letter and he said he didn't believe a word of the story.

"You know what you are, Stretch?" he asked. "You're a liar, the world's biggest. I don't think you ever threw a baseball in your life. Maybe you was the bat boy. You'd make a good bat boy, Stretch, because you're bats." He laughed, doubling himself over in his chair.

I could see Stretch feeling bad because he was proud of those baseball days of his.

"Shut up, Arthur," I said.

"What did you say, professor?" he asked, the laughing choked off.

"I said: 'Shut up,' " I answered, pleased I'd gotten a reaction out of him. "Let me tell you a secret, Arthur, that everybody knows but you. Know what we call you behind your back? Awful Arthur. Awful Arthur. Know why? Because you look awful and you smell awful and you *are* awful."

He couldn't believe his ears, and to tell the truth, I couldn't believe my own either because I was never too brave without a drink in me.

He got up and kicked a chair and we all watched it fly against the wall and bounce into a corner. He started pacing the floor, seething with anger because he couldn't do anything about my insults: I was an older man and he couldn't hit an older man. At least I was counting on that. He looked so miserable pacing the floor, without a friend in the world, that I started to feel sorry for him. He was still a young man, wasting his life, and the only thing he had to be proud about was his strength. Mr. Jones kept him busy doing the heavy work, moving furniture or pushing cars that got stuck in the winter, and when Awful Arthur was called on to use his strength you could see him performing like an artist on a stage, proud of himself.

But his strength was all in his legs and hips and that's what gave me the idea: looking at his thin arms, I knew that I could arm wrestle him easy if I put my mind to it. We used to wrestle with our arms a lot of times at Lu's Place and I won my share of contests, sometimes against big men like Jean-Baptiste La Chapelle. Even though I felt sorry for Awful Arthur in his pent-up fury, I felt worse for old Pete Honiker and Stretch and even for myself because, who knows, I might have become a professor one time. I thought: He needs to be taught a good lesson, that's what he needs, and maybe he'll start treating us like human beings.

So I challenged him to an arm-wrestling contest and he couldn't hide how happy he was once I convinced him I meant business and began to roll up my sleeve. He figured it was a chance to get revenge on me, on all of us, I guess.

Excitement shivered in the air as we sat ourselves at a table and put our elbows down on the surface. Suddenly, I was the happiest man in the world. The geezer sat opposite me and the men stood around like a cheering section, encouraging me, and I felt like a young man again, a full fresh breeze at my back. We placed our hands together, clasping each other, and Stretch yelled out, "Go," like an umpire calling a long strike, lengthening the word, and I curled my legs around the chair for leverage and girded my muscles and I felt brave and gallant and like a hero, you might say. But I was barely ready when Awful Arthur's hand tightened around mine like a vise and he forced my hand back on the table so hard and fast that you could hear the crack of my knuckles like a pistol shot.

"He wasn't ready," Stretch complained. "You didn't wait for him to get set . . ."

The geezer laughed quietly and old Pete hollered, "Get him this time, Tommy, fair and square." The geezer chuckled because he knew, all right, that he beat me fair and square. "Okay, let's try it again," he said, and you had to admire him with those skinny arms and those terrible eyes.

I squared myself once more, trying to bring strength all the way up from my toes. I pitched all my power into my arm and we locked hands and he knocked my hand down as if it was straw. I got up from the table fast and the room was so quiet you could hear a lawn mower far away, and an awful feeling of being lonesome came over me. But I'll say this for the geezer: he didn't gloat or anything. He seemed happy, for once. He settled back nice and easy in the chair and said, in a soft hoarse voice: "You're okay professor, but it's thirty years too late . . ."

Suddenly Mr. Jones poked his head in the door.

"Tommy," he called. "Can I see you a minute?" I would have given anybody a million dollars for getting me out of that room at that minute. And it made me feel important to be called special, all by myself, by Mr. Jones.

"Pardon me, gentlemen," I said, as nonchalantly as I could. I knew I had let them all down and I felt extra bad for Stretch, who was shaking his head as if he'd lost a no-hit game in the last of the ninth inning.

Mr. Jones and I walked down the hall toward the men's toilets, and he stopped me with a hand on my arm. "I just got word," he said. "Sweet Mary's dead. She died of the pneumonia . . ."

Rage shook me, thunder and lightning. My heart started to beat in a wild way, as if a bird had gone mad in my chest, and I made a dash for the toilet door and barely made it inside in time. I sat there, weak, thinking: I'm tired of everything, tired, tired of everybody dying, always dying. I was tired of double pneumonia and gallstones and cancer and sugar diabetes and strokes and heart attacks and blood poison and cars hitting people and all the rest. Everybody's always dying, I thought, everybody I ever knew.

The room spun around for a minute and then settled into place. I breathed deep and I guess the stuff they used to wash the toilet, to disinfect everything, kept me from fainting; it was stronger than smelling salts, even.

"You all right, Tommy?" Mr. Jones called from outside.

I told him I was fine, just a touch of the flu probably, and asked him to go away and let me be for a while. After a few minutes I heard his footsteps fading slowly down the hall.

Then I felt bad because I hadn't given a thought to Sweet Mary. I'd only been thinking of myself. But it's just as well she died, I thought, consoling myself by remembering that she was alone in the world and didn't have a friend and they didn't even want her to smoke her cigarettes and nobody cared whether she came or went and it was just as well she died of the pneumonia because she'd have burned to death sooner or later, smoking her filter cigarettes in bed.

After a while I went out into the hallway. Harold came down the hall and I looked away from his pimples, wondering whether they would turn to cancer someday and kill him.

"You all right?" he asked.

"I'm all right," I told him.

"That's too bad about Sweet Mary," he said.

"I want to go to her funeral," I said.

"You sure you're all right?" he asked again. "Mr. Jones was worried about you. He's up in his office calling long distance about Mary and said to see if you're all right . . ."

"I want to go to her funeral," I said again.

"You can't go to her funeral. The body's going to be shipped out to Illinois. That's what Mr. Jones is calling about. That's where she came from, can you imagine that? All the way from Illinois and she ended up here. They got the body at the funeral home waiting for the next train out . . ."

I don't know. I started feeling worse—about Sweet Mary being all alone in the funeral home waiting for the train, no wake, nobody sitting around in a parlor talking soft or some others in the kitchen telling jokes and old stories like they do at wakes and saying how nice she looks, all fixed up with flowers around her and reciting the Rosary when the priest comes by.

"All right," I said.

Harold shook his head. "Her funeral." He touched my shoulder. "You're a funny old guy . . ."

"So funny I could cry," I said.

"**T**HAT'S TOO BAD about Mary," Stretch said, standing beside me on the veranda that evening, "dying like that . . ."

The sun had gone down and twilight softened everything. I looked at the road to town as a car roared by, the headlights pulling it along.

"That's not going to happen to me," I said, not looking at him, wishing he would leave me alone because he made me think of how Awful Arthur had beaten me in front of everybody and how I had let them all down.

"We all got to die sometime," Stretch said.

"Not here," I answered. "Not in this place. They're not going to take me out of here feet first. I'm going to die *on* my feet downtown . . ."

"No matter where, it's all the same," Stretch said. "It's coming to all of us, Tommy. None of us are young any more. We're all old."

"What's age got to do with it?" I asked, anger making my voice loud in my ears. "A man is as young as he feels. Why, I got a friend getting married day after tomorrow and he's almost as old . . ."

"You're just getting restless, Tommy," Stretch said. "Maybe you ought to take a couple of days off, get away from here for a while . . ."

They let you out sometimes on weekends or on holidays or on special occasions if you signed the register and told where you were going, visiting a relative or a friend or an old neighbor. But I didn't have any relatives left and I didn't want to visit any of my friends while I was living at The Place. Besides, it riled me that a man had to sign his name and tell where he was going and have them lock the door at ten o'clock at night. If you were late and Mr. Jones had to let you in, they took away your outside visiting privileges for three months.

Sweet Mary's money, that sixty-three dollars, kept coming to my mind. It was more than I'd had in my hands for a long time, enough money to get a fresh start.

Somebody called for Stretch to play a game of pinochle and he trudged away. I stood alone in the twilight thinking how nice it would be to walk off the porch suddenly and down the road, without looking back.

Old Pete Honiker was out on the lawn plucking dandelions as usual. Every evening when the dandelions started to wither as if they were tired from a day in the sun, he'd go out and start digging away at them with an old fork Mr. Jones had given him.

"Come on and help me pull up these dandelions, Tommy," he called. "I want to get this front lawn done tonight . . ."

I was glad he wanted my company after the mess I'd made of the contest with Awful Arthur and I thought: What the hake. So I went down to him and knelt; and there we were, like a couple of damn fools, pulling up the dandelions.

I said: "You might catch a cold on this wet grass, Pete."

"Naw," he said, businesslike, his hands working steady, "You only catch cold in the water, a tub or a pond."

"How come you don't like dandelions?" I asked. "They're kind of pretty if you ask me . . ."

He thought about that for a while. "I don't know," he said, shrugging. "I just don't like them. I don't like butter, either . . ."

I was going to ask him what butter had to do with dandelions except when you hold them under your chin to see if you like butter but he looked up at me suddenly, grinning, his thin old face wrinkled in the dim light so that he looked a hundred years old.

"Ain't this nice, Tommy? You and me picking dandelions together . . ." he said.

The motorcycle boys drove by at that moment, the headlights sweeping our faces, and I wondered if I looked a hundred years old, like Pete, to the young fellows going by. I thought to myself: Here I am on my knees on the lawn of the poorhouse picking dandelions, and I don't know why I'm doing it and the fellow who invited me to help him doesn't know why he's doing it, either. I felt as if The Place was beginning to affect me, the way it had already affected old Pete with his crazy battle against the dandelions and his hate for taking baths, and Stretch who still mooned about some old letter he lost maybe forty years ago, and Awful Arthur always aching for a drink, and even Mr. Jones who had those ghosts following him around.

And I decided once and for all to leave The Place, to take Sweet Mary's money, more money than I'd ever expected to have at one time, and leave.

A cool breeze freshened my face and confidence waved in me like a bright banner.

"Pete," I said, "let's have a dandelion-picking contest. See who can pick the most . . ."

He looked at me carefully, measuring me with his pale eyes, and they lit up like fireflies, and he giggled: "Okay, okay . . ."

We talked over the rules and he insisted that the roots had to be dug up or it didn't count and he shyly pulled a fork out of his pants pocket, looking around to see if Mr. Jones was nearby because, he explained, he'd swiped it from the kitchen to use as a spare. Anyway, we started digging up the dandelions, both of us scrabbling away on our knees, our hands flying like birds, getting all green and yellow and dirty. "You're going to need a bath tonight," I joshed him. "We're getting all dirty . . ."

"I don't care, I don't care," he said, all excited and happy as he pulled at the dandelions.

After a while, some of the men and women came out on the veranda and Pete yelled at them over his shoulder, not missing a stroke of work: "We're having a contest, we're having a contest . . ." They gathered around us, and Annabel Lee was with them, jumping up and down with excitement, and it was nice, in a way, in the gathering dusk with all of them calling to us, and Annabel Lee's happy laughter, dancing like silver on the air, and the women giggling, and the men cheering us on and everybody happy.

When the contest was over because of darkness, they picked Harry Herman to count the dandelions. He did it slow and easy, all puffed up with the women around because he was always a man for the ladies, and I sat back against a tree, tired and happy. Pete won by a ridiculous amount, way ahead of me, and I was glad for him: it didn't feel the way it had when Awful Arthur knocked down my arm. He cackled with glee and punched a couple of fellows on the arm, so happy he was, and then he squinted at me and came over, formal and serious, and put out his hand. "No hard feelings, Tommy? I mean, I've got more experience at it than you . . ."

The bell rang inside the house, announcing that it was time to get ready for bed, and Stretch and I walked back together. I took him aside and told him I was leaving The Place.

He kind of chuckled, shaking his head.

I knew what he was thinking and I didn't blame him in a way. Many's the time I'd told him how someday I would leave The Place and I guess he must have gotten tired of hearing the story and figured that I was just talking. But now I explained about Sweet Mary's money, all that money in my bureau drawer, and suddenly he wasn't smiling.

"You're really going then?" he asked.

"Tomorrow morning," I said. He turned away and kicked at the veranda like a little boy.

"Why don't you come along, Stretch?" I asked. "I got enough money for both of us . . ."

"No, I can't go, Tommy," he said.

"Why not?" I argued, and yet all the time I argued with him I was wishing he wouldn't come because I wanted to go alone and I wanted to leave everything and everyone at The Place behind.

"I'm too used to it here," he said. He turned toward me and his face was all lines as if sharp claws had gouged him. "It's not bad at all here. We got everything we need. I remember when you first came . . . you didn't even want to *talk* about downtown. And anyways, what are you going to do down there, an old man all alone?"

I closed my eyes and I could see it all, like a moving picture in my mind. "I'm going to get my old job back, that's what," I said. "I'm going to be with people and get a nice place to live in with no rules saying when you have to go to bed, and maybe buy a television and stay up at night watching the late, late movies without somebody saying to put out the lights and go to bed . . ."

"I'm sorry I can't go, Tommy, honest," Stretch said.

Somebody called from the house, telling us to get in there, and I stomped away from Stretch without saying good night. I took a bath to wash the smell of The Place out of my pores. Afterward, I walked down the hallway and saw little Annie kissing Mr. Jones good night and felt bad for a minute, thinking of those Saturday mornings and how I should have written that letter to the newspaper about her. I went to my room and put on two of everything: two pairs of socks and two shirts and two pairs of pants, the old Khaki pants for working and my good brown herringbone-tweed trousers to wear nights and Sundays. I crammed my polka-dot necktie into my back pants pocket and took out my nice green-plaid sports jacket that always cheered me up when I saw myself in the mirror, and hung it over a chair so that it would be ready the next morning. I put my little black book in the jacket pocket. I didn't bother with anything else because I wanted to travel light and buy new clothes when I got settled down. I planned to sleep in my clothes and slip out quietly the next morning before anybody woke up, because I wasn't going to sign any register as if I was on parole from a prison. I was going to leave for good, without looking back, burning my britches, like they say.

I took out Sweet Mary's money and counted it. There were ten five-dollar bills and five two-dollar bills and three ones. The money was old and slippery, and smelled of stale perfume and tobacco. I put the bills in my wallet and placed the wallet under my pillow. Once in bed, I pulled the blankets up to my neck so that my clothes wouldn't be seen if someone happened to come in.

For the first time in weeks, sleep came like a soft hand stroking me, settling comfort on my bones, and my dreams were sweet although I couldn't remember later what they were, just that I slept with a sweetness all around me in the dark.

Until something startled me from sleep: the sound of running and a muffled cry and a feeling of emergency. Rubbing my eyes, I looked at my alarm clock—four o'clock, the night still black at the window. I got out of bed, surprised to find myself all dressed up, and then I remembered my decision to leave the infirmary. Voices echoed from one of the men's wards, worried and tense, and I felt whatever was happening was a threat to my going away. I hurried down the corridor and met Mr. Jones rushing out of a ward. He looked ridiculous in his pajamas, *silk* pajamas with Chinese dragons jumping all over them, and the sweat was pouring out of him, a drop of perspiration perched at the end of his nose.

"It's Stretch," he said. "I think he's had some kind of attack. The doctor's on his way . . ."

I wanted to slam my fist against the wall even if I broke my hand doing it. For a moment, I didn't care about Stretch or what happened to him, whether he was sick or not, because I knew that my plans to leave The Place were changed, that I wouldn't be able to escape, not with Stretch there in bed, sick and maybe dying.

Then I cursed myself for my selfishness because Stretch was a good friend, and he thought I was a fine man, and that always made me feel like trying to be a fine man.

"I'll go stay with him," I told Mr. Jones.

"What the hell's the matter with you?" he asked. "You're all dressed up—and you look lopsided, all out of kilter . . ."

I looked down at myself and remembered I had on two pairs of everything but there was no way I could explain it to him. Then Stretch started moaning in the ward and Mr. Jones forgot all about me and we went into the ward to stay with Stretch until the doctor arrived.

BUT I LEFT the place after all that day.

First of all, it turned out that Stretch wasn't seriously sick. The doctor said he'd suffered an attack of acute indigestion, and he warned him not to eat cucumbers for supper any more. Stretch lay on his bed, weak from all the vomiting and his cheeks gaunt and pale.

Mr. Jones came in that morning fussing and fuming, his eyes red from his broken sleep. He was annoyed because he had to go to Boston to attend a meeting of infirmary superintendents and he said it was unreasonable to have a meeting of that kind the day before a holiday, especially Memorial Day.

"I got all those flowers to bring around to the cemeteries," he said, "and I promised to take Annabel Lee to the graves and here I am going to Boston . . ."

Every year the city provided bouquets—not flowers, really, but plastic wreaths made into the shape of flowers—for the residents of the infirmary. Everybody there was allowed one wreath to place on the grave of a loved one, and Mr. Jones went around to the cemeteries the day before Memorial Day, delivering the wreaths so that on the holiday itself, the graves looked nice when the people at The Place visited the cemeteries after the parade. Annabel Lee loved to arrange the wreaths on the graves because she didn't have any conception of the fact that dead bodies were under the green grass.

Mr. Jones cautioned Stretch to stay quiet and asked me to keep an eye on him and I went out to see him off. He kissed Annabel Lee on the cheek and told her he'd buy her a present in Boston and that cheered her up a little although she couldn't hide her disappointment.

"I'll try to get back late this afternoon so I can get to the graves before dark," Mr. Jones said as he lunged into the car, jamming his hat on his head. His collar was starting to wilt. He shifted gears too fast and the motor screeched as the station wagon shuddered. As he approached the end of the driveway, the motorcycle fellows came along in a formation, two by two, and there were twelve or fifteen of them strung along the highway. Mr. Jones raced his motor impatiently, waiting for them to pass. But they didn't pass. They drew up across the road at the old pump, spraying dust as they skidded to a stop, the wheels spinning and the motors roaring as if war was declared.

Mr. Jones blew his horn and shook his fist at them, but the motorcycle boys didn't pay any attention. They were all dressed the same way that day, in some kind of uniform— black leather jackets that had pictures of a white eagle on the backs, military hats like the soldiers wear, and black goggles hiding their eyes. Mr. Jones kept blasting away with the horn but they took their time, pulling up to the pump in a deliberate way, most of them hidden for a while behind clouds of dust. Finally Mr. Jones drove out onto the highway, his own tires squealing and kicking up dirt.

Minnie took Annabel Lee into the house, telling her that she could help make the chocolate pudding for lunch, and I went up to the ward to see Stretch.

He looked sadder than ever lying there in bed.

"I'm sorry I got sick, Tommy," he said. "You'd be downtown by now if it wasn't for me . . ."

"I can leave any time," I told him. "After all, I couldn't desert a friend. And what difference does a day or two make, anyway?" But my heart wasn't in the words, really, because I was afraid that something would always stop me from leaving. I looked at the plain white bureau that stood beside his bed, the shaving bowl with dried soapsuds clinging to the sides, and the glass of water holding his false teeth. As soon as he was on his feet, I promised myself I would leave.

"I hope I don't miss the Memorial Day Parade tomorrow," he said. His eyes moistened. "I want to visit Lou's grave, too, and see the flowers there . . ."

"I wouldn't be surprised if you were up and around tomorrow," I said. "After all, a little indigestion is nothing to stop a man."

He nodded but didn't look any happier. I knew by his expression that he was still thinking about Lou. You could tell when he was thinking of her because a gentle sadness crossed his face, the sadness that I'd seen when he sat in that barber chair at night. When I saw that look on his face, I wanted to tell him that it was no use thinking of dead people, whether you loved them or not. A man gets to be a certain age and he knows more dead people than live ones, and there's no good in thinking of them because you can't bring anybody back and memories only make you feel worse. I had tried to bring back all my dead people, especially Sophie, at one time or another, and you never can, no matter what you try, liquor or prayers or wishes.

After a while Stretch started to get restless; he kept moving around in the bed, trying to find a comfortable position.

Finally he asked me if it would be all right to go down and sit on the veranda.

He tested his strength, sitting up and dangling his legs over the sides of the bed, and I helped him get dressed and then held his arm and we walked that way to the veranda. Harry Herman offered to let Stretch sit in his favorite chair, a big lawn chair that was the only one Harry had ever found to accommodate his big behind.

Harry wandered off to the back of The Place where the men were laying out the horsehoe squares for the summer and Stretch and I sat there quietly together. A terrible belch rolled up out of his stomach once in a while.

The sky was filled with clouds, big round clouds that looked like scoops of vanilla ice cream although every so often the sun got covered up and the air turned cool. I remembered how Sophie and I used to sit on the piazza in the evening while we were waiting for the baby to be born and I'd go down to the corner and buy her an ice-cream cone and wouldn't even glance at Lu's Place.

I tried to make myself turn from the thoughts because sooner or later the sadness comes. I heard the screen door slam and saw Minnie coming out on the Veranda. There was something shattered in her eyes as she told us that Annabel Lee was missing.

The worst thing in the world is waiting, whether it's waiting for a baby to be born in a hospital where nobody pays any attention, or waiting for somebody to die and you can only stare out a window at a store awning sagging in the rain, or waiting for a lost girl to be found.

Some of the men began to search the nearby fields, calling Annabel Lee's name and the wind lifted their voices and sent them through the air like ghost sounds. The women hunted all over the inside of the infirmary, led by Pete Honiker because he knew all the hiding places. I stared out across the road where the motorcycles had been.

Knobby came up after a while, his big black eyes wide with fright. He looked pale beneath his brown skin.

"We ain't found her yet," he said, as if I didn't know.

"They won't find her in the fields or in the attic, either," I said.

"You got some special information?" Harry Herman asked, joining us, wiping his face with a Kleenex.

"She never goes out to the fields," I said, not wanting to mention anything about the motorcycles yet. "Mr. Jones always warned her about wandering out there and she never disobeys him. And if she was in the attic she'd have heard us by now, all that hollering . . ."

I was hoping the motorcycles would come along before I had to tell them.

"Two things bad," Harry Herman said "two things. First of all, if she'd just wandered off and disobeyed for once and gets into any kind of a bad fix and the Board hears about it, there'll be trouble. The city won't let her stay here anymore . . ."

I looked up at him, hating him as he stood there talking. There are some people in the world who enjoy emergencies, who get a strange pleasure out of something bad happening, but I'd never thought Hungry Harry was one of them.

"The other thing," he said, "is if she meets with an accident. Terrible, terrible. It'll kill Mr. Jones. Just kill him outright . . ."

He sat down on the steps, taking about two minutes to get

his big stomach arranged just so, the stomach filled with food he'd never paid for or worked to get.

"So you see," he began again.

"Shut up," I said, cutting him off.

"What's the matter with you?" he complained, looking hurt.

"I'll tell you what's the matter with me," I answered. "Those motorcycle boys. I think they took Annie away. Maybe for a ride. She was telling me the other day that one of those fellows asked her to take a ride and she almost went. I warned her about it but you know how she is. She thinks everybody in the world is innocent like her." I kicked at the veranda step and hurt my foot. "I should have told Mr. Jones about it. He'd have done something about it, and she always minds him . . ."

The sound of a motor reached our ears, fast and furious, coming closer all the time. We turned our heads in the direction of the sound but it was only a car, one of those small foreign cars, brilliant red, making as much noise as a Mack truck.

"The motorcycle riders were here this morning when Mr. Jones left," Stretch said. "I could hear them all the way up in my room."

"Looks bad, looks bad," Harry said, his thumbs hooked into his belt.

Minnie came back, her face red and perspiring, and she looked on the verge of tears. She shook her head, her hair askew, one lock of gray hair falling over her forehead. "She's nowhere around here," she said, "nowhere. I was just thinking . . . those motorcycle fellows were here this morning . . ."

"That's what we were just discussing," Harry said.

"Tommy said she had a yen to go for a ride on one of those things, and one of the fellows even asked her once . . ."

"Yes, she told me about that," Minnie said. "And I should've known better than to leave her go out this morning. But she was restless, disappointed about not going to the cemeteries, and out she went. And a while later I heard the motorcycles leaving . . . and she must have gone with them." She burst out crying, lifting her apron to bury her face in it, her big shoulders shaking and heaving.

"Don't feel bad, Minnie," I said. "It's not your fault. She maybe just went for a little ride around the corner . . ." But my voice didn't sound too confident.

"Don't look on the black side of things, Minnie," Harry Herman said. "What we've got to do is to sit down and figure this out. We've got to keep calm and cool and take it easy and figure out something . . ."

What we had to figure out was this: getting Annie back safe and sound, and doing it without raising too much of a fuss.

Harry took charge. First, he calmed Minnie down. He was the one who did all the figuring and you had to admire him, the way he could lay out the problem, plain and simple, and take charge of things, although you could see that he was enjoying it all. I mean, he was concerned, all right, and worried like the rest of us, but he seemed glad that there was something unusual going on to break the monotony of the routine and I thought that it was a shame he had decided not to work because he had a good mind, and you could almost see his brains clicking as he talked.

"Two things," he said, motioning us to move closer to him so that he could lower his voice. "First of all—secrecy.

The more people know about this, the worse it'll be because word is sure to get out and this whole place will be in an uproar. Right now, most everybody probably thinks she's just playing some kind of game, like hide-and-seek, and nobody but us is really worried . . ."

You had to hand it to him. His voice was matter-of-fact and businesslike, and even Minnie paid attention.

"All right. So, Minnie, in a minute, you march right in The Place and tell everybody that you found where she is. Tell them you called the farm next door, I think somebody by the name of Peters runs it, and tell them Annie is over there, visiting. That'll stop the panic . . ."

"I think we ought to call up the police," Stretch said. "This is dangerous business, Harry. No telling what those wild fellows will do and she might even get in an accident . . ."

Harry looked disgusted.

"You going soft in the head?" Harry asked him. "Look, we got no guarantee anything's happened to her. She might come riding up with them any minute, and once the police are in on this, the whole city'll be in an uproar and they'll probably send her away to that special school down near Boston . . ."

"He's right, Stretch," I said.

" 'Course, I'm right," Harry answered. "You've got to take the long look at things. I took a long look at things forty years ago and never did a bit of work since and look at me." He patted his big stomach. "Anyway, we wait one hour for her to come back. It's broad daylight and nothing too much can happen in broad daylight and there must have been fifteen or twenty fellows there on their motorcycles. Safety in numbers, Stretch, safety in numbers."

Stretch nodded finally and I could see the logic in what Harry was saying. I kept looking toward the highway, trying to convince myself that I could hear the roaring of motors coming closer.

"Second of all," Harry said, warming up to his job, the relish and enjoyment coming back into his voice, "if she don't come back, we look for her . . ."

"How can we look for her?" Minnie asked. "Go traipsing out on the highway?"

"We go traipsing nowhere," Harry answered. And I saw what he was getting at.

"The telephone," I said. "We use the telephone to look for her . . ."

Harry looked at me, smiling. "You're all right, Tommy," he said. "I can see why they call you 'professor.' " He turned to Stretch and Minnie. "Now look, a bunch of motorcycles makes quite a lot of noise and it's hard to hide them, I'd say. So—two things: first we call the state police barracks that's between here and Worcester and we don't tell them who we are but just inquire if some motorcycles have been by there. Those state police can radio to any of their cruising cars. And then we call downtown and ask them the same thing. And we keep calling, the police in Litchfield and the state police barracks they got on Route 2 on the way to Boston . . ."

"But what do we do if they tell us they've seen them?" Minnie asked.

Harry frowned and looked toward me and I didn't know what to say. It seemed like the police would have to be told about the situation.

"Let's cross that bridge when we come to it," Harry said. "Besides, the state police have got nothing to do with the town. They can probably track them down and get Annie back here and nobody will be the wiser . . ."

It didn't sound too convincing.

"Well, least we can do is get started right away on the telephone calls," Minnie said. "It's not ten o'clock yet, and we'll give ourselves that hour you mentioned . . ."

"Good," Harry said. "Let's make the phone calls before we get all mixed up in the details. Then we'll have another talk and decide what to do . . ."

Minnie went off to tell the people that Annie had been found and Harry Herman waddled off to make his telephone calls. I told them I would stay on the steps, listening for the return of the motorcycles.

"Take it easy, Tommy," Stretch said. "It's not your fault . . ."

Stretch was a sad old man and nobody ever gave him too much credit for brains, but it seemed sometimes as if he had a gift for looking deep inside people.

"They're downtown," Harry yelled from inside the infirmary, his heavy footsteps flapping on the floor as he rushed toward us. He pushed the screen door open with his huge stomach and he was excited. "The police station says that those motorcycles have been driving everybody crazy for the last hour or so, buzzing in and around the main streets, and causing a traffic jam because there's a lot of people out shopping for the holiday . . ."

"Did they see Annie with them? Did they happen to see her?" Stretch asked.

"I didn't ask them about Annie, man. That'd give the whole thing away. I was going to ask them if there was a young girl riding around with them but I thought that might get them suspicious."

Harry hooked his thumbs in his belt again and his trousers sagged below his big stomach. He was pleased with himself. "Things look pretty good, I'd say. The danger is cut way down. Way down. I mean, it's safer to have her riding around town with them than out on the highway somewhere or some lonesome road. So I think we can relax a bit . . ."

"Relax?" I asked. "I'm not relaxing until she's back here safe and sound . . ."

"What's going to happen to her downtown?" Harry asked. "They're just giving her a big thrill, that's all . . ."

I stood up, tired of just sitting there and talking. "Look, Harry," I said, "you figured it out all good and I give you credit for that. Maybe what we're doing is wrong, not telling the police, but I figure it's worth the chance so that we don't do anything to spoil things for Mr. Jones and Annabel Lee. But I'm not just going to sit here and wait for her to get back, not when I've got two good legs and some money in my pocket. I'm going downtown after her . . ."

"Tommy, that's a smart idea," Harry said, snapping his fingers. "Why, you can call a taxi and get there in fifteen or twenty minutes and find her and bring her back in no time . . ."

I frowned, stirred by a small whisper of guilt: did I really want to go downtown for Annabel Lee or was this an excuse to leave The Place after all?

"I'd sure feel better about it if you went," Stretch said. "Otherwise, there's no telling when they'd bring her back . . ."

"Okay, Tommy," Harry said. "I'll go inside and tell Minnie and have her call a taxi. No use wasting any time . . ."

Stretch looked up at me and smiled in a funny way and I turned away, wondering if he was thinking that I was really leaving for my own reasons and not only for Annabel Lee.

"Tommy," he said. "Would you walk with me up to the ward? There's something I want to get . . ."

I helped him up and held his arm as we went along. When we got to his room, he searched in his bureau for a while, pulling out all his clothes, not looking at me, and then he found what he was looking for and turned toward me.

"Here," he said. "This'll keep you safe . . ."

It was a St. Christopher medal.

For crying out loud, I wanted to tell him, I'm not taking an automobile trip across the country. But his old pale face was so thin and sad that I only said, "Thanks, Stretch."

The Town

• • • • • • • • • •

It DIDN'T LOOK like a taxi at all, except for a shiny silver aerial stretching above the roof: an old car, maybe twenty-five years old. The new red-plaid seat coverings clashed with the smell of decay and the wet stains on the faded green upholstery of the ceiling. I thought of the taxi that Sophie and me took to the hospital the night she died, an old Buick.

"To town," I said to the driver, trying to be jaunty but depressed by the old car and angry that it should be spoiling my departure. I waved to Harry and Minnie who stood on the steps of the veranda, both of them looking uncertain and worried. Harry shouted something at the last minute but his voice was lost as the driver shifted gears and drove off in a cloud of dust.

The driver was a young fellow, about thirty, and he drove with one hand, chewing the fingernails of his other hand, and that depressed me, too.

"Nice day," I said, "although there's a feel of rain in the air . . ."

He grunted, hunched over the wheel, chewing away at his fingernails, concentrating hard on something and I hoped it was the road.

The night Sophie died: a hot night, the night before the

Fourth of July, and everybody walking through the streets as dusk crept in, heading out toward Carpier's Park for the big bonfire, and firecrackers exploding on the sidewalks, as the young fellows tossed the two-inch salutes toward the feet of the passing girls. And the girls always squealed and screamed and stuck their fingers in their ears. Sophie cried all the way and I did too, and the crying made the driver nervous so that he kept jerking the car, and it seemed as if the car was gasping and sobbing too. She was a month early in her pains, and bleeding, and she was old to have a baby, almost forty-two, and there was no ambulance in town and we drove to the hospital in the taxi, clinging to each other all the way, the sweat smell of her getting stronger all the time, and I wasn't able to comfort her or even put my arms around her, she was so big with the baby. She gained thirty-five pounds carrying the baby and she was a big woman to begin with.

"Is this a Buick?" I asked the driver, my voice sounding thin and high, something of a scream in it.

The driver turned and looked at me in surprise and the car swerved a bit and he turned around to the front and shook his head. After a while, he said: "Chevy," still shaking his head.

I have a trick of turning my thoughts aside, of not thinking about the old days and the things that happened, good or bad. But I was afraid that the trick wouldn't work. The taxi made me sad, those poor wet stains on the ceiling. I lit a cigarette, the match jumping in my hand as we bounced over the road.

I didn't go home for two days after Sophie was buried.

Cut that out, I told myself. Think about Annabel Lee, think about downtown, think of today, this minute, not anything that happened a long time ago.

I leaned forward, putting my arms on the top of the front seat. "You know where the motorcycle boys hang out downtown?" I asked.

He didn't answer for a minute. "Look, mister," he said, still chewing away at his fingernails, working hard on his little finger, "I got my worries, you got yours." He shook his head again. "Is this a Buick. Boy . . ." At least that had got a chuckle out of him.

I settled back in my seat and noticed we were passing a new housing development, rows of small houses looking as if they'd been made by some giant cookie cutter. Small children played on the lawns and some women in shorts were watering the grass with hoses.

"They got a place near the city dump where they race around," the driver said at last, squeezing the words out of his mouth.

"Thanks," I said, sarcastic as I could be with only one word although I can be pretty sarcastic at times.

"Lots of the boys driving around town today?" I asked.

He sighed, annoyed. I could see by now that he wasn't a very friendly fellow. "Yeah, they're around," he said.

"Thanks," I answered, putting more sarcasm into the word but he didn't seem to notice, too busy chewing away. It gets me mad when you are sarcastic to somebody and they don't pay any attention.

We were getting close to the city and the land was flattening and losing its prettiness. We passed empty lots with junk strewn around and small factory buildings and big billboards. Then I saw a monument, a tall thin stone like a pencil pushed into the ground and the point sticking into the air. The name of this town is Monument, like I probably mentioned, and the people here are crazy about monuments, feeling maybe that they have to live up to the name of the place. Every time something happens, like the year the high school band won the marching contest in Boston or when somebody important dies like old General Weatherbee who fought in the Spanish-American War, up goes another monument. They even started renaming the streets after the Second World War, giving them the names of famous battles. The city pays a fellow a special salary to keep all the monuments in town clean and polished up, and the mayor once hired an expert from New York to solve the pigeon problem. I've got no quarrel with monuments, but there are some terrible sections of town that should be cleaned up, the old tenement buildings torn down and the people given new places to live in. Anyway, there are all these monuments all over the place, honoring everybody and everything except the really big war, World War Two. Funny thing. Ever since the war, the town had argued about what kind of monument should be put up to honor the fellows who fought—and it almost started a war in Monument. One faction was getting tired of statues and such, and wanted to add a new wing to the public library, but the other faction wanted to put up the biggest and highest monument ever erected. I'd heard they finally settled on another statue but a man gets foggy about details living in a place like the infirmary. It seemed to me that I'd heard they were going to dedicate the new monument on Memorial Day and I'd have asked the taxi driver about it but I didn't want to bother him. And I noticed, anyway, that we were driving into the business district, past the stores and apartment buildings leading toward the square, and I began to think again of the motorcycles.

"Where you want out?" the driver asked.

"Anyplace. Right here," I said.

He pulled up to the curb in front of an appliance store and I paid him. I didn't feel much like tipping him, to tell the truth, but he held out his hand and I saw those chewed-up fingernails.

"Seventy-five cents," he said.

I gave him a dollar and said: "Keep the change."

He didn't even thank me.

Downtown.

The sights and the sounds. The people and the traffic. The stores and the buildings. The green haze of maple and elm hanging above the Common. The colors and the smells. The windows dazzling with sun. And everything hustling and bustling. Cars honking and traffic lights flashing. The Memorial Day flags tossing in the air as if they were trying to get free from the light poles that held them back. The red-white-and-blue bunting flapping on the fronts of buildings. The men and the women and the children, and baby carriages and bicycles and shopping baskets from the supermarkets. The bright gay dresses on the women and the crazy-colored sport shirts on some of the men, and a high-school girl gliding by in orange shorts. Everything and everyone moving, even the buildings seeming to shimmer in the clear morning light, and a burst of music as a young fellow came along carrying one of those transistor radios you hear about, gaudy fast music keeping time to the throb of my pulse.

Oh, downtown, where the good times are.

You can have your holidays: I always liked the day *before* the holidays, when the people are out shopping and some of the factories let the workers quit early and there's an air of something happening, something promised, something good that's coming.

I'm never going back to The Place, I said to myself as I began to walk toward the center of the business district where Main Street widens out to form a triangle, the place where all the fancy stores are and where the Common sits on the north side of the triangle, like a proper old grandmother, calm and serene.

A little girl in pigtails that were all askew and coming apart dashed across the street, between cars and trucks and reminded me of Annabel Lee. You've got to find her, I told myself; there's nothing more important right now.

A young fellow in a brown leather jacket and wide side-burns on his cheeks approached and I stopped him. He looked like a motorcycle rider himself.

"Say, fellow," I said. "Have any of the motorcycle fellows been riding around town here?"

He smiled at me. "You a rider, pop?"

I get riled when people call me pop or old-timer or things like that, judging a man by the gray in his hair, but I let the remark pass because Annabel Lee was more important.

"No," I said. "I'm just looking for them. I got a nephew rides one . . ."

The lie rolled easily off my tongue and it kind of surprised me. I used to be quite a liar in my time and I'm still pretty good when I'm in the mood. I used to lie like a trooper in the barrooms because everybody expects things to be exaggerated when you're drinking. But hadn't done much lying at The Place: there didn't seem to be any reason for it. I was glad to see I was still in practice, though.

"You got me, pop," he said. "Seems I saw some drive through a while ago but I can't say for sure . . ."

I thanked him and walked away in a hurry. The hurrying made me feel better although I didn't know where to go, exactly. I mean, where does a man begin to look for motor-cycles?

There is a small traffic circle in the middle of the business center and I saw that there was a new monument in the circle, if you could call it a monument. It was a kind of shaft, made of brass and wire, bronze and gold, and there was one of those modern clocks at the top, an electric device that writes out the time in numbers, like 11:10, changing every minute. As I looked, the numbers changed from 11:10 to 11:11 and there was something terrible about that clock, showing you how fast the minutes go by. I realized that Annabel Lee had been missing for about two hours and I had an urge to go to the police station and ask for help.

A cop who had been directing traffic headed in my direction.

"Pardon me, officer," I said as he drew near.

He was an older cop with a weather-lined red face, the kind of cop you picture munching an apple he'd lifted off a fruit stand. He wore big dark sunglasses, though.

"Do you know where I could find those fellows, the ones who've been riding motorcycles all over this place this morning?" I asked.

"They been in and out of the square all morning long," he answered, "driving everybody crazy. They give kids too many vacations these days—a whole week off at the end of May when they're going to start summer vacation in a month. But the cycles haven't been around for the last half-hour or so . . ."

"Know where they might be?" I asked. "A fellow told me they have a racing place out by the city dump . . ."

"Could be there now," he said. "They've got some kind of meet this afternoon, in Medford, out near Boston, and they usually get together at that field near the dump, making up their formations before they go."

"Thanks a lot, officer," I said, drawing away from him. The news about Medford chilled me and I was afraid I'd blurt out the whole story.

The city dump was at the end of Mechanic Street about two miles away. It was ridiculous to think of walking all that distance and I looked around for a taxi stand. I chuckled in a sad way: I hadn't taken a taxi since the night Sophie died and now, inside a half-hour, I'd be sitting in a taxi again.

I remembered that there used to be a stand next to Sweeney's Diner around the corner on Elm Street, and I walked there without wasting any more time, hating to glance at that new modern clock that clicked away the minutes so fast. There was an old clock on the top of the Congregational Church on the other side of the Common but the tall trees hid its face.

Sweeney's Diner wasn't there anymore, the place where I used to stop by for a hot dog after the movies at night, but I didn't have time to feel bad about that or to wonder why they had to tear down a nice, respectable place like Sweeney's to put in a parking lot. The taxi stand was still there, though, and a driver sat in one of the cars, reading a paper.

"Can you drive me out to the dump in a hurry?" I asked, sticking my head in the window.

He was a middle-aged fellow with thick glasses that magnified his eyes. "The dump? In a hurry?" he asked, putting down his paper.

"That's right," I said.

Ordinarily I would have explained the situation to him but I was getting a little tired of fresh taxi drivers.

"Hop in," he said, tossing the newspaper aside. "You want

to go to the dump, I'll take you to the dump. You planning on coming back?" he asked, and he started to shake with laughter, coughing and sputtering and getting a big kick out of his joke, if it was a joke.

"And make it snappy," I said.

"You bet your life," he said, racing the motor as he waited for the traffic to clear so that he could pull out into the street. "I always rush people to the dump fast. Yes sirree, whenever anybody wants to go out to the dump, I notice they're always in a hurry . . ."

He fancied himself a comedian, I guess, but I didn't enjoy his brand of humor at the moment although I like a joke as well as the next man. In fact, I didn't enjoy the ride at all. Mechanic Street was familiar to me, especially the section between Fourth Street and Seventh Street where I spent most of my years. Under ordinary circumstances, I would have enjoyed riding past, looking at the stores and the buildings and the tenement blocks, but my mind was on Annabel Lee and nothing else.

"Stop here," I said when I saw a field a few hundred feet before the dump. The field looked like an improvised race track with no bleachers or fences or anything.

"This isn't the dump," the driver complained, acting disappointed.

I didn't answer. There wasn't a motorcycle in sight and the dirt in the roadway part of the track looked untouched, the gravel undisturbed.

I kept looking at the track and the driver cleared his throat and drummed his fingers on the steering wheel.

"There's nobody there," I said, the panic beginning in me again.

"You okay, mister?" the driver asked, looking like a frog with the thick glasses resting on his puffed cheeks.

You could smell the burning from the dump: there was always a fire smoldering there, the smoke hanging low as it spread across the street like a disease.

"I was looking for the motorcycles," I said. "I've got to find those fellows."

"Hell, why didn't you say so in the first place and save yourself a trip?" he asked, friendly now. "They're all gone. They took off maybe a half-hour ago for Medford. Big doings out there. A big meet at two o'clock . . ."

"Did you see them go?"

"See them go?" he asked. "Who the hell in town didn't see them go and *hear* them go?"

"Did you notice if they had a girl with them, a girl riding on the back of one of those motorcycles?"

"A girl? You must be kidding, mister. They all had a girl. Who they going to show off for if they don't take their girls along? I'll tell you one thing—no daughter of mine'll ever ride on one of those bikes. There's enough other ways to get killed than trying that crazy stuff . . ."

He wasn't cheering me up at all.

"Look," I said, "how far is it to Medford? Forty miles? Can I hire you to take me out there?"

"I'm sorry, mister," he said, turning back to his wheel. "No wild-goose chases for me. Besides, I'm quitting early today 'cause the wife's relatives are coming for the holiday . . ."

"Better take me back to town," I said, my stomach getting tight. "I've got to make a phone call . . ."

* * *

Minnie answered the telephone, her voice high and strained. "Minnie," I said. "It's me, Tommy Bartin. Look, Minnie, those motorcycle fellows aren't downtown . . . they've all gone to Medford."

"I know," she replied. "Mr. Jones is here. He called the police . . ."

"Mr. Jones? How come he's there?"

"He came back fit to be tied. He had car trouble out on the highway and said to heck with the meeting. And we had to tell him, Tommy. There was nothing else to do. So he called the police . . ."

Poor Mr. Jones. "Was he mad at us, Minnie?" I asked.

"He was too worried to be mad. He called the police and they told him about the motorcycle boys being out in Medford and said they'd get in touch with the police out there. And they told Mr. Jones to stay put here and wait. And he's locked himself up in his office and I think he even took a drink out of that bottle he keeps in the safe for emergencies. He won't talk to anybody and he told me to answer the phone and not bother him unless it was about Annie . . ."

I was thinking how a good shot of whisky would unravel the knots in my stomach and warm my bones. The sky had clouded over and the street looked bleak and lonesome, people hurrying along and glancing up at the sky now and then, getting ready to dash for cover if the rain fell.

"Now listen, Tommy, you better get back here. Did you have any dinner yet? It's after noontime and I'll bet you haven't had a bite. You better hop in a taxi and come right back here. I got that nice spicy meat loaf you love and I'll heat some up for you . . ."

"I don't know, Minnie," I said. I didn't want to hurt her feelings any but to tell the truth I never liked her meat loaf too much, because I like dishes that have a lot of gravy, but I never let on, always praising her cooking since that was the big joy of her life. "We're still not sure Annabel Lee's out in Medford with the motorcycle fellows and maybe I should stay down here and keep my eyes open . . ."

"The police put out a bulletin on her," she answered. "She's a missing person now. The police are looking for her, even downtown. So you better come back, Tommy. There's nothing you can do about it now."

"Well, Minnie," I said, "it took me three years to get here, and maybe I'll stay down awhile. See some of my old friends . . ."

"All your friends are up here at The Place, you know that," she said. "You've got no business being down-town . . ."

The anger flashed in me again, heating my cheeks and throbbing at my temples. She sounded like Stretch, thinking that the whole world ended at the bottom of the driveway at The Place.

"Tommy," she said, her voice sad, and that stirred my anger even more because everybody at The Place was so sad that a normal man could hardly stand it.

"Look, Minnie," I said, impatient to get away from her voice, "to tell you the truth I've got my old job lined up. And I've got enough money to get me by. I've been thinking of not going back at all . . ."

"You've got a short memory, Tommy Bartin," she cried, her voice stiffening the way it did when you started pestering her in the kitchen. "I guess you don't remember how disgusted you were three years ago when you first came here, how you said you were going to turn your back on the whole world. Those were your exact words, your own words, not mine. You said you were tired of being stepped on. Remember that, Tommy Bartin, remember that?"

"What the hake, Minnie. I was sick and just got out of the hospital and had too much to drink at the time. It's different now . . ."

"The world doesn't change, Tommy. And if it does, it doesn't change for the better . . ."

The street had gotten darker and the wind chased a torn brown paper bag down the sidewalk, and a young girl tripped along, hugging her skirts to her thighs. I thought to myself: Maybe Minnie is right, maybe Stretch is right, too. What am I looking for downtown? But I couldn't answer the question in words. It was something inside that seemed to be talking to me in a foreign language, not even a language really but in some strange tongue that had no voice, no words. And all I knew was that I had to stay downtown, that I had to put The Place behind me.

"Tommy, you still there? You still there?"

"I'm here, Minnie," I answered. "And I'm going to stay here." My voice sounded loud and strong and confident—too loud, perhaps, because a young fellow sitting at the ice-cream bar in the store turned and looked toward me.

"Tommy," she said.

It was a terrible thing to do but I banged the receiver on the hook, to shut off her voice. I thought of The Place: Stretch mooning over his dead Lou, and old Pete Honiker hiding to keep from taking a bath and Awful Arthur tortured for a drink and Harold Hennifer bursting out in tears for no reason every once in a while and even Minnie herself who looked like Joe Palooka's mother but was a lost soul outside her kitchen and Mr. Jones with his ghosts following him and poor Annabel Lee who could break your heart just by look-

ing at you. I stepped out of the booth feeling as if I had
turned away from a cold, windy precipice that had been
ready to suck me down into blackness.

My clothes were still at The Place but they weren't much
anyway. I could buy some new duds after I got a job. And I
was wearing my Sunday best, my nice green-plaid sport
jacket, and my honeymoon tie and my white shirt. Sweet
Mary's money was in my wallet and my little black book
was in my jacket pocket. And maybe Frenchy would be in a
good mood and hire me back . . . and there was the Memorial Day parade tomorrow and Charlie Morrissey's wedding and reception.

I stepped out of the drugstore and the sun flashed bright
again, and I felt as if I was home once more, standing there
on Mechanic Street, money in my pocket and nobody in the
world to tell me what to do.

And who knows, I thought. Maybe Annabel Lee is somewhere downtown and I might find her and be a hero, not
only to The Place but downtown where it counts.

MECHANIC STREET is long and it stretches all the way from the town line at the dump to the business district uptown where you'll find the fancy stores and City Hall and the public library and the Common full of monuments where I used to sit on summer evenings, watching the people going by. But the part that was *really* Mechanic Street, the part you thought of when anybody mentioned the name, was a small section, maybe three blocks long, with St. Jude's Church at one end and Lu's Place at the other. It's funny that the church and the saloon should be located that way. My mother always said that God was at one end of Mechanic Street and the Devil at the other.

Between the church and the saloon was the shopping area, the small stores on the street level and the tenements above, most of them three stories high, with piazzas looking out over the street. The people used to sit out on the piazzas on spring and summer evenings, after supper, swatting at flies and cooling themselves with those cardboard fans showing pictures of pretty girls that Suprenant's Drug Store gave away with a quart of ice cream.

I looked up at the piazzas. The afternoon shadows were gathered behind the fancy railings and it seemed suddenly like it was fifty years ago, as if time had fallen asleep behind the banisters and nobody had grown old or died or gone away. . . . The women would go to church in the evening, strolling on the sidewalk in the twilight, past Suprenant's and Gorgier's Meat Market that always had those food specials on big, white sheets of wrapping paper pasted on the window, the words scrawled in red crayon; past Renault's Billiard Parlor where the kids hung out until they saw their mothers coming; past Allain's Department Store that had only one department, Dry Goods. The men always sauntered toward Lu's Place, meeting their friends near the mailbox across the street, and loafing there awhile as if the last thing on their minds was stepping across to Lu's for a few cool ones. Finally they walked to the saloon and pushed through the door, stepping into another world, a world of loud talk and arguments about baseball and the work rates at the shops . . . and a man could let himself unwind a little, although the wives could never understand that. Even Sophie never liked me to spend too much time at Lu's Place.

Old Mr. Gorgier kept his market open until about quarter past nine every night, and when he walked past the store, carrying his little package of scraps for his dog at home, that was the signal for most of the men to leave the saloon, if it wasn't Saturday night. You'd hear the voices of the women on the dark, cool air, calling the kids into the houses, the voices somehow sad in the soft, still evening. The married men would begin straggling out of the place, finishing their beers slowly, savoring the last dregs and wiping the foam from their lips, trying to act casual as if they had all the time in the world, as if they weren't really in a hurry to get home before the wife made a fuss and sent one of the kids after them. Then they'd swagger out of the place, pretending there wasn't any rush, and you could see that they hated to leave, just when the evening was commencing. It's funny, though. Before I married Sophie and after she died, I used to stay in Lu's Place after the other fellows left, the married ones, and it was never as nice as they thought it would be if they'd stayed. I wanted to tell them that sometimes, tell them that they ought to be glad to get home to the wife and kids, but you never can tell anybody things like that.

All those thoughts came to my mind as I stood on Mechanic Street that afternoon but I realized that the old neighborhood was gone, really. Not only the people but the buildings themselves. There was a parking lot with meters where Suprenant's Drug Store had been, and Renault's Billiard Parlor was now one of those laundry places where people put a coin in a machine and wait around for the washing to be done. A supermarket, all chrome and glass, had taken the place of Gorgier's Market. Old Gorgier was a small fellow, a whisper of a man, but he had a kind heart and couldn't refuse credit to anybody during the hard times. He finally moved away, almost overnight, leaving all those unpaid bills still owed to him, because people found out one day that he used to trick little girls into his back room.

My father didn't like the old Gorgier even before he knew about the little girls. They argued through the years because of the way the grocer spelled my father's name. Our family name is really Bartineau and my father was proud of his French-Canadian heritage and could talk about Canada and the small parishes on the banks of the St. Lawrence River until people got fed up and said to him: "For God's sake, why didn't you stay there?" Anyway, Mr. Gorgier always spelled my father's name this way: Bartino. And when he handed my father the bill on payday my father would explode in anger.

"Bartino? I'm not an Eyetalian," he'd bellow. "Do I ever buy spaghetti? I'm one hundred per cent French first, and right after that I'm an American . . ."

Once, my father won the turkey that the grocer raffled off each week and he stuck my father's name up in the window: Theophile Bartino. The next day my father went to City Hall to have his name legally changed to Bartin.

I think my mother was relieved that he changed the name. In the first place, she hated arguments in those days although her tongue got sharper as she grew older. But when we were young, my mother wanted to turn her back on Canada and told my brothers and sisters that we were Americans first and French second, no matter what my father said. She wouldn't let my father speak French at home and made us all read and write in English. She took special pains with me because I was the youngest and she started me in the habit of writing things down. When my mother and I were left alone after everyone else had died, she'd have me read aloud to her in English and it was only then that I realized she couldn't read a word of English herself.

Anyway, I stood before Gorgier's and started feeling bad about everything, my father and mother and everyone dead and even the old Gorgier himself. And I got angry and kicked at a telephone pole, disgusted that I should start missing somebody like him who did terrible things with little girls, and that's why I don't like to remember too much, because you find yourself lonesome for everything, even the bad things.

A bus came along the street, and somebody waved from the bus, sticking an arm halfway out the window. A voice called: "Hi, Tommy . . ." I squinted against the sun, catching the blurred image of a smiling woman, a young woman's face pressed against the window. Nobody like that had waved at me or called hello for a long time and I watched the bus as it lumbered past, hoping it would stop and that the young woman, whoever she was, would leap down the steps and come running to me, although I couldn't imagine anyone who would do a thing like that.

I kept watching the bus and it didn't stop, of course, and I started down the street in the direction of Lu's Place, thinking of that face in the window, and then I suddenly remembered. The young woman was Harry Breault's wife, Emily, and there was this letdown, a disappointment in the remembering. What I mean is this: for a minute there, it might have been anybody in the world, maybe somebody lost who was finding me again, something impossible and yet at the same time possible, something wonderful although there was nobody lost in my life, nobody like a young woman who would wave at me from a bus. But when I realized that it was Harry Breault's wife, the impossible stayed impossible and the sweetness went away. Not that I didn't like Emily: she was a fine woman. She and Harry and their two kids, two little girls, lived on the second floor of Miss Bein's apartment house where I used to have a room, and sometimes I'd sit with the kids, taking care of them while Harry and Emily went to the movies or spent an evening visiting friends.

Miss Bein owned a big apartment building on Spruce Street, four stories tall, with two or three tenements on each floor, and it was filled with young couples and their children. People called it "The Beehive" because there was always somebody coming and going, some excitement buzzing with all those people living there together. The police cruiser used to drive up about once a month when Henry Therrialt got drunk and started throwing furniture out of the third-floor window, and old Mrs. Tellereux used to hide her garbage in the milk boxes of other people, but it was a nice place to live, full of life and things going on. I went to live at Miss Bein's place after my mother died because our five-room tenement on Sixth Street was too big for a man alone and I didn't know anything about making beds or keeping a place clean and I always had the feeling, during the weeks I lived there by myself after her death, that my mother would walk into the room some morning and wake me up like she used to. Sometimes in that quick time before I woke up, during that moment when you are between sleeping and awaking, I half expected her to walk into the room and touch my shoulder and this sweet ache would fill my chest although I knew I would drop dead on the spot if she ever did that.

Miss Bein didn't want to rent me a place at first. She was a nice old Jewish woman with a thick accent and she could burst into tears at the drop of a hat because she was so sentimental. She had a whining voice that sounded like the tail end of a howling wind blowing in her chest. Anyway, she didn't want to rent me a place because I was interested in a little room at the very top of the building and she said that walking up four flights of stairs would kill me. Finally she gave her consent, but she used to stand at the bottom of the stairs watching me start up, shaking her head and sighing in a mournful way and watching me so close that I started worrying myself about having a heart attack. I used to rest at every landing and it took me about an hour to climb up to my room because after a while I got to know the people in the building and would stop and chat with them in the hallways and had a fine time.

I was happy living there in "The Beehive" with all those people, glad the walls and ceilings were thin as early winter ice because you could hear everything going on without feeling guilty about eavesdropping, and it kept my mind busy. Harry Breault and his wife were my best friends there, although Harry was always too worried about himself to be real friendly with anybody. He was a walking medicine cabinet with pill bottles in his pockets, and that was funny because he was a big man and weighed over two hundred pounds. Emily used to baby him. I think he was always sick because he liked to be babied, and Emily seemed to enjoy treating him that way. Their little girls were nice children and they never gave me any trouble when I sat with them in the evening except they hated to go to bed because I'd read them jokes and my "ladies and gentlemen" poems from my little black book and they could have listened to them, over and over again, all night long.

Often, I'd go downstairs to the sidewalk and sit on the small cement wall at the bottom of the front steps and chat with Miss Bein. She lived on the first floor and she'd sit at her window. She was the saddest woman I ever met, sad even when she laughed at my little jokes, and she was always talking about the old country although her accent made her stories hard to follow. Sometimes I didn't pay attention to what she was saying and I'd only listen to her voice that sounded like a lullaby, soft and crooning, when she told her sad stories.

Miss Bein's sadness was different from the kind you find in a place like the city infirmary. She seemed to enjoy a good cry the way other people like to hear jokes. When I realized that Miss Bein liked to be sad I helped her along, asking questions that would start her on her sorrowful memories and telling her about bad news I'd read in the newspaper or heard at the shop, and you could see her eyes get pert with interest while her mouth started turning down at the corners. Sometimes I'd make up the bad news, if all the news happened to be good that day, and old Miss Bein would moan and cry and have a good time, really.

As I stood there on Mechanic Street after the bus went by, I decided to go over to Miss Bein's apartment and ask for my old room back. I thought how nice it would be living there again, with all the excitement, and kids dashing in and out, and Miss Bein listening to those sad stories in the evening.

I hurried along the street to get there fast because the people passing me by were strangers and I wanted to talk to somebody familiar. A fellow came along wearing bright green shorts, his hairy legs bare except for green garters holding up his socks. I shook my head, thinking that only women should wear shorts, if anybody has to wear them.

I turned the corner and saw Miss Bein's apartment house, four stories high. Imitation brick covered the old gray paint and there were shiny aluminum frames around all the windows. A happy feeling came over me as I stood there because I figured Miss Bein must have inherited some money from a relative and used it to fix up the place.

Inside the first-floor hallway, I knocked at the door and waited. A young woman opened the door, all dressed up to go out, a handbag dangling from her arm and a small brown beret on her head.

"Yes?" she asked, frowning as if she thought I was a salesman or somebody like that.

Suddenly I knew I shouldn't have come.

"Pardon me," I said, saying the words automatically, because I already knew the answer to my question. "Is Miss Bein in?"

"Oh," the woman said, her face softening. "She's dead.

She died two years ago, suddenly, just came in the house one day and set her table for supper, and had a heart attack . . ."

You're a foolish old man, I told myself as I hurried down the street. You come back after three years and expect everything to be the same, no changes at all. You act as if the whole world stood still while you've been at The Place, as if everybody was waiting like statues for you to come along and blow on them and breathe some life into them.

I was dying for a cigarette but I was afraid to light up, knowing my trembling would scare the life out of me. I thought of what Minnie had said about downtown and I stopped walking and leaned against a light pole and closed my eyes to shut out everything for a minute. I'm not going back, I said to myself, I'm not going back. It's just that a man has to be given a chance to get used to things.

I opened my eyes and looked up the street and remembered that Lu's Place was only two blocks away. I thought: I'll drop in there and have a beer or two because everything always feels better with a couple of beers singing inside and by the time the beer begins to work I can call the infirmary and they'll tell me that Annabel Lee is back, safe and sound, and I'll go see Frenchy and get my job back and everything will be morning again.

THERE'S ONLY ONE WAY to enter a saloon and that's to walk in as if you had a million dollars in the bank and could buy the place, lock, stock and barrel. I've been in a lot of saloons and barrooms and cafés and no matter if I was feeling happy or blue or had only the price of one glass of beer I always walked in with my shoulders swinging and my chin tilted, pushing the door open quick as if I had things on my mind and other places to go. That way, people are glad to see you and they want to talk to you and have you stay awhile.

So when I arrived at Lu's Place that they now call the Golden Rooster although there's no sign of a rooster anywhere, no sign at all in fact, I automatically spruced myself up, getting ready for my entrance.

And I also braced myself because I knew there would be a lot of changes inside, and I wanted to get ready for them. Lu had died a long time ago and I hadn't stepped into the place for many years because I had always dreaded the people I *wouldn't* meet, the people that wouldn't be there anymore.

The dark coolness of the inside, after the bright hot sun, made me squint. I peered around as I advanced to the bar and saw that there were a lot of changes, all right. The old wooden tables and chairs were gone, replaced by some fancy plastic-covered booths, bright orange. There was a big painting of a golden rooster over the bar above the mirror and the rooster didn't look too friendly: it didn't seem like a friendly kind of picture to have in a bar.

Two young fellows were sitting at the bar, quietly drinking beer and studying a newspaper spread out before them. They glanced up as I sat down and looked away without interest. The bartender was busy polishing glasses, his back turned to me, and I waited for him to turn around but he kept right on working. Finally, I coughed to let him know he had a new customer and it spoiled it all, having to cough that way to let him know I was in the place.

"Oh, I didn't hear you come in, pop," he said, turning around. I didn't mind him calling me *pop* because bartenders have to use nicknames like that, they see so many people. And, anyway, he looked familiar: his hair was slicked back with glistening stuff on it and his eyes had small laugh wrinkles in the corners and he looked like Lu himself. A good feeling spread over me.

"You must be Lu's boy," I said, although he wasn't a boy, but maybe twenty-five or thirty years old.

"Lu . . . that was my grandfather," he said.

A shiver went through me: the cool bar after the hot sun outside. I figured I would have a shot of whisky along with the beer to warm myself.

"He was a good man, your grandfather," I said.

"I don't remember him much," the bartender said, still wiping a glass. "What'll you have, pop?"

"Yes, he was a good man," I said, remembering. "He used to make elderberry wine but he never sold it over the counter. He always kept it for special occasions like the night before Christmas, and he'd bring it out and give us all a drink on the house . . ."

He stood there, nodding his head, in that patient way of bartenders, listening and yet not listening. "What're you going to have?" he asked.

"A little shot," I said, "to take away the chill. And a big beer for a chaser. A shot and a tall . . ." I made up a poem once about that shot-and-tall stuff and wrote it down in my little black book and it was kind of funny, if I do say so myself, and I was kind of tempted to recite it to him but he looked preoccupied, all those glasses to wipe, and I didn't say anything.

He poured the beer and the whisky and placed the glasses before me on the bar and I paid him. I lifted the whisky and watched the way the light caught at the amber. I thought of Awful Arthur back at The Place, that terrible thirst of his, and I almost lowered the glass. Here I was, not really needing a drink but taking it for pleasure, and there was Arthur back at the infirmary agonizing for a shot and he didn't have any. But I drank it down and then reached for the beer to take away the raw sting of the liquor in my throat.

The first drink in more than three years . . . the beer was cool and oily and clinging, the way tap beer always is, and the taste freshened my throat and cooled my stomach. I was glad that the beer tasted the way it always did, like an old friend who hadn't changed, and it felt nice to be sitting on that orange plastic bar stool.

The two fellows were still studying the newspaper, figuring out the races, I suppose, and the bartender was busy at the end of the bar, bringing out a broom and dustpan. I sipped the beer again, swishing it in my mouth, and I could feel the lull going through me, the way it always did, softening my bones and muscles, like a soft hand stroking you from the inside.

It was quiet in the place with only the muttering of those two fellows and the swish of the broom on the floor and I began to feel lonesome. I never liked quiet saloons, the way they are early in the afternoon or in the strange, still time around supper hours when everybody else is at home eating or reading the paper or fooling with their kids. I liked to see a lot of people in the place, arguing and talking, and a kid coming in to sell a newspaper, and somebody making a bet about how many home runs Babe Ruth hit in a certain year, and the music playing, a piano in the old days and a jukebox in the later years, and the bartender patiently filling those glasses and sending them sailing across the top of the bar, like an artist. And the smell of the men: you could always tell where the men worked by the way they smelled, the celluloid from the comb shops and that ironing-board smell from the shirt shops and the sawdust tang from the piano-case factory and the gritty smell of grease from the machine shops, all mixed in together with the smell of beer and sweat, the smells enough to make you drunk by themselves.

The two young fellows got up and left, without saying a word, not like in the old days, when the best part of the time was leaving, stopping here and there at a table and joking with the bartender. And I brought myself up short, thinking: You've got to stop comparing, Tommy, or you'll get to be like everybody else at The Place, living in memories.

But I was getting more lonesome by the minute and my glass of beer was empty. I saw the jukebox in the corner, quiet and dark, and thought how nice it would be to hear some music.

"Is the jukebox connected?" I asked the bartender.

He sighed and shook his head and walked in a very tired way to the jukebox and stuck the plug in the wall. The lights came on but the little neon tubes were cold and didn't start to bubble the way I liked to see them. "I got a lot of work to do," the bartender said, but not cross or anything.

"A man's got to have a day off once in a while," I said. "You ought to ease up a bit. That's why I took today off, tomorrow being a holiday, and I've been working overtime . . ." And while I was talking, I was thinking to myself: My God, you've started already. There's something about a saloon that always turned me into an awful liar, the lies streaming out of me at sixty miles an hour, not lying exactly but a kind of pretending.

"The boss is going to be mighty unhappy when he sees my machine standing idle today, but what the hake, a man needs a day off once in a while, isn't that right?" I said, unable to stop the words from coming out of me as I walked to the jukebox. Actually, I wasn't lying or even pretending: I was just borrowing from days gone by, when I *used* to work every day and even sometimes at night and took a day off once in a while. Just borrowing to show the bartender that I wasn't a drifter, that I was an important man at a shop.

He didn't answer me but started to pick up the sweepings in the dustpan. "I used to come here all the time," I said, "before I moved to the other side of town. That's why you don't know me . . . I've been living up there quite a while. Everybody used to know me. I'm Tommy Bartin. Maybe you heard of me . . ."

"The name sounds familiar," he said, walking away, carrying the sweepings and I never heard a bartender say anything different when he didn't know a person.

I put some money in the jukebox and didn't even pick out

a special tune because the titles all sounded the same and I didn't recognize any of them. This terrible music started to blast out of the machine, an inferno of sound, crashing around the bar, but at least it was something to fill the place up, to take away the emptiness.

I tapped for another beer, hitting my glass with a coin, and the bartender drew me a new beer and placed it before me. I drank it quickly, swallowing most of it in one gulp, and I didn't pay him for the beer, making him wait for the money. That's a trick you learn when you drink in a lot of bars and want somebody to talk to: you don't pay the bartender but hold the money in your hand and he stands there waiting and it gives you a chance to strike up a conversation and maybe get him interested.

He was standing there, all right, waiting, and I tried to think of something to say quick but we didn't have much in common, really, to talk about since we'd never seen each other before. I noticed then that he had a little red poppy in the lapel of his white jacket, one of those imitation poppies that the veterans sell.

"Say," I said, happy for a topic, "they going to unveil that new statue tomorrow?"

"Yes, pop," he said, looking at my fist that held the money. You couldn't blame him for being suspicious because some fellows are always trying to get a drink when they haven't got a dime in their pocket.

"So they finally decided to put up a monument with all that money they been raising the last ten, fifteen years," I said, knowing I would have to pay him in a minute because you can't push that kind of thing too far.

"Yeah, this town needs a new monument like it needs an

atom bomb dropped on it," he said. "Thirty thousand dollars for a lousy statue . . ."

He was still eying me closely so I handed him the coin. He rang it up and started to shine the glasses again. The beer was beginning to work, helped by that shot, and a nice warm feeling came over me and my head got a little light but it was pleasant and the music filled the place and then it stopped and I figured I had better go see Frenchy before it got too late. And yet I hated to leave the place, really. There is something nice and friendly about a saloon: some of the best times in my life happened in a saloon. But the bartender turned his back to me again, busy with the glasses, and I finished my beer and got off the stool.

"It was nice talking to you," I said. "It's been really pleasant . . ."

He was working away at the glasses and a truck rumbled by and he probably would have said good-bye to me but he didn't hear me, I guess. I stepped outside and blinked against the sun and the street slanted foolishly for a minute and my stomach dropped a couple of inches inside of me like it happens in an elevator and I leaned against the doorway to support myself. The sun affects me that way sometimes when I leave a saloon. A little girl walked by, licking at a yellow lollipop, concentrating on that lollipop, yellow for lemon, for all she was worth and her face was scrubbed and shining and she was wearing a bright, red dress and the sight of her cheered me . . . and I thought of getting my job back and how I had left The Place behind me and it seemed that all the nice things in the world were waiting for me somewhere, just around the corner.

The funny thing is that you know it's the beer talking, whispering to you, and that a lot of times the feeling is a fake, a thing of the moment, but it doesn't change the good things at all. And I thought: Now, right this minute, I'm going to see Frenchy and when I call the infirmary in a while to inquire about Annabel Lee I can tell whoever answers that I've got my job back and that I'll never return to The Place.

Frenchy's shop was a two-story building with peeling, faded paint that was at the end of a narrow driveway in the rear of a big automobile repair shop. As I started up the driveway, my foot kicked a broken whisky bottle. I halted in my tracks, looking down at the bottle, not wanting to look up.

Funny, but I sometimes think there's a mysterious man who goes around breaking bottles all over the world, smashing them in the yards of houses that have been abandoned, or in back alleys where nobody goes but stray cats and dogs, or in the driveways of buildings that are closed and boarded up, all the windows broken and the chimney bricks loose and crumbling. You know how they're always breaking a big bottle of champagne when a new ship is launched, how the newsreels show the bottle going *smash* and the pretty girl leaps back so she won't get splashed and the ship starts to slide slowly down the chute and everyone cheers and waves? Well, I think the same thing happens in reverse when a place closes down, when the people go away, when the door is closed and the windows shuttered: a mysterious man comes around and breaks an empty bottle, a whisky bottle usually, to mark the place . . .

"Oh, no," I whispered, looking at that bottle at my feet.

My head still down, I walked up the driveway to Frenchy's and, finally, raised my head and looked up at the old shop where I had worked forty-five years and the building seemed like a blind old man sitting there, waiting for somebody to come along and pass a miracle.

There was no sign of life. The air was fresh and clean without that dry, sweet-acid smell of the plastic powder they put in the molding machines. The windows weren't broken and somehow that was pleasing to see and I thought: Maybe it's vacation time, maybe Frenchy has shut down the place only for a week or so although he never believed in shutting down, even the day before Christmas. Then I saw the wooden plank nailed across the door, like an old Band-Aid, dirty and stiff.

I saw a slip of paper nailed to the door and walked up the warped wooden steps. The floor of the platform was scarred with cigarette burns from the times when the workers stood there having that last puff on a cigarette before the whistle blew. I squinted at the words on the paper.

"Closed indefinitely. Call at Atty. Solomon Blaum."

And somebody had scrawled with a green crayon down below: "Go to hell."

Harold answered the telephone and he got excited as soon as he heard my voice.

"That you, Tommy? That you? Listen, Tommy, you left without signing out. Do you realize that? You're supposed to sign the register when you leave . . ."

His voice irritated me but I kept myself calm because I didn't want him bursting out in tears. "Harold, it was an emergency when I left. Mr. Jones knows I'm gone . . ." I looked out at the square, the buses pulling up and people getting off, in a hurry to go someplace. There was a fellow with a pail of water washing the park benches and people would come along and test the benches to see if they were dry and then they'd sit down. "And besides, Harold," I said, "I'm not coming back, anyway. I'm staying downtown . . ."

"Are you crazy, Tommy? You're always getting me into trouble. You have to sign out to leave permanently, have to fill out forms and everything. And I'm the one who gets blamed when the forms aren't filled out proper. I'll bet there's a law somewhere that the Board'll dig up about signing out in emergencies, too . . ."

"Well, anyway, I'm staying downtown," I said, surprised really by my words. When I'd left the shop building and headed for the center of town, I hadn't known what to do. I knew it was impossible to live away from The Place without a job and I'd tried not to think about it, using my old trick of keeping my mind away from what was bothering me. But now as I stood in the telephone booth in the center of town with all that activity filling my eyes and ears again, I knew that I couldn't go back. I watched that fellow washing the benches, sloshing the water around in a sloppy way, and I figured: There are all kinds of jobs in the world and there must be someplace for a man with my experience: all those years at the machines and the timekeeping job I'd held.

"Mr. Jones is going to hit the roof," Harold said, his voice trembling.

"Look, Harold, if it'll make you feel better I'll take a taxi back to The Place sometime next week and sign all those forms. But right now I want to know what's happened up there. Is Annabel Lee back? Did the police locate her in Medford?"

"Oh, they found her, all right. She was with those motorcycle boys, sitting up in the stands, eating a Popsicle. Mr. Jones has gone after her now, and he's going to be raving at me when he comes back. Why didn't you and Harry and Minnie tell me what you were planning? There you went, sneaking off behind my back and getting me into trouble . . ."

"I'm sorry, Harold," I said. And I was sorry in a way but I couldn't really open up my feelings for him because I kept staring out of the booth at all the sights, the comings and goings, and I opened the door of the booth a bit to hear the noises better. A little boy dressed up like a grown man, in a blue suit, a soft hat on his head, stood at the bottom of the veiled statue, pointing up at it while his mother explained what it all meant. And I wondered what the statue looked like and told myself: Well, I'll find out tomorrow morning after the parade and I won't be standing with a bunch of old sad people being supervised by Harold or Mr. Jones. I'll stand where I want to stand.

"You better get back here, Tommy," Harold was saying, "and forget all that foolishness about staying downtown. Officially, you're up here. That's official. Suppose you got hit by a car or had a heart attack or something? I'd never hear the end of it. Mr. Jones is upset enough about Annie without you being a fugitive from . . . from justice, for goodness sake . . ."

Poor Harold. The more he talked, the more he convinced me that I would never go back. I glanced at the men and women on the park benches, taking their ease in the sun and watching the people going by, and thought how nice it would be to sit there for a while, resting and deciding about the future: where to find a job and a room to stay and which restaurant I would choose to eat dinner in (I was starting to get hungry because I hadn't eaten since breakfast) and it was pleasant thinking of all those decisions to make, all these things to think about.

"Look, Harold," I said, "you tell Mr. Jones I'm sorry to leave him in the lurch and say that I'll drop back sometime and sign those papers. And tell him, Harold, to please put that bouquet of flowers on Sophie's grave down at the cemetery and I'll pay him back later, as long as I'm not living at The Place anymore . . ." I was planning to visit the graves in the morning when the paraders marched there although I seldom went to cemeteries: the stones and the grass and the little flags seemed to have nothing to do with the bodies underneath and the bodies seemed to have nothing to do with the people that you used to know and love.

"Tommy, you can't do this. The rules say you've got to follow procedures . . ."

My eyes had been looking over the Common, sweeping the scene in an absent way, and suddenly I saw a familiar figure slouched on one of the benches. I squinted, pressing my face close to the window, and saw Baptiste, my friend from the old days at the shop, a friend from the times of long ago. I got all excited.

"Well, Harold," I said. "I've got to go now. I just spied an old friend of mine and I've got places to go and things to do. You give everybody my best regards and tell Mr. Jones I'm glad he found Annie . . ."

"All right, Tommy," Harold said, the fight all gone out of him. I don't think Harold ever won an argument in his life or expected to. He had a few more things to say but I wasn't listening to him, really. I was looking at Baptiste, hoping that my eyes hadn't deceived me, hoping that it was really him.

"So long," I said to Harold when he stopped talking. I was impatient to get away from the telephone, afraid that Baptiste might suddenly get up and walk away before I could cross the street. I left the telephone booth, lifting my face to the fresh clear air but keeping my eyes on my old friend on the bench, glad that Annabel Lee was safe and sound, and my britches burned behind me and that was enough for the moment.

His FULL NAME was Jean-Baptiste La Chapelle but everyone always called him Baptiste (pronouncing it in the old French way: Bah-teece), and although he'd lived in Monument most of his life his accent and big awkward figure gave the impression that he had left the farm in Canada the day before yesterday. His hair had always been so black there was the blue of bruises in it and his eyebrows were bushy enough to comb and his smile wide as a sunrise.

I pumped his hand happily and was glad that he didn't get up from the bench because he always towered over me, making me feel small and puny.

"Hallo," he said. "How you be?"

He was awful with the English language, getting his words and sentences mixed up. I once filled a whole page of my little black book with his sayings but I never showed it to him or anybody else because he was a proud man.

"I thought you went back to Canada when you retired from the shop," I said. He didn't invite me to sit down and I was kind of glad because there was a big wet spot right next to him on the bench, a puddle the cleaning man had missed wiping away.

"No sirree," he answered, shaking his head. "I was go down to Canada and come back quick for good. . . ."

He didn't look at me but stared out across Main Street, puzzling over something. I glanced in that direction but didn't see anything special, just the people and the stores and cars passing. He was frowning away, the two mustache-eyebrows touching each other over the bridge of his broken nose. He broke that nose when he did a drunken dance one night on a table at Lu's Place and went hurtling to the floor, dizzy from spinning too much. I took a close look at him. His hair was thinner and turning gray and the shape of his jaw and lower cheeks had changed, the way they do when you start wearing false teeth.

For a minute I was sorry that I had met him again after all those years. It would have been better to remember him when he was the champion rubber of the comb shop. The rub room was the hardest place to work in the shop, a filthy room where the men sat like dwarfs bent over the speeding wheels against which they held the combs to smooth away the rough spots. The wheels spun in a trough of wet ashes, a gray, foul-smelling mud that stopped the combs from heating up because of the friction. Mud splashed everywhere and the roar of the machines and the smell of sweat and ashes choked the air. But Baptiste never hunched over the wheel like the others. He had long, fence-post arms and he sat upright on the stool, like a king on a throne. He rubbed the combs happily, chewing a big, unlighted cigar, and you could hear his booming voice and his hoarse bellow and laughter over the noise of the machines. He was an ugly man with a rough, pockmarked face but you never thought of him as ugly or good-looking, only as Baptiste.

"Now, all the time I thought you were back in your old hometown, retired and enjoying the good life," I said.

He shook his head emphatically. "No good down there. I

grab my money when I leave the shop and went down Canada and walk all the street in the town where I was born but the place was fill with everyone who ain't there no more . . ."

See what I mean about the way he talked? I was itching to pull out my little black book and take notes. "You mean everybody you knew was gone away?" I was getting tired standing there and having to look down at him but that puddle on the bench hadn't dried up yet.

"Oh, the people there all right," he said, looking up at me at last. "Know where I find them? Six feet down in the *cimetière*. I go to the *cimetière* and read all those name on the stone, all my friend from the longtime days, and there they are, six feet down. I kneel for one minute, and put some ground on my hand and I think: Ground we are and ground we going to be, like it was say in the Bible. . . . So I come back here where at least I don't feel such a stranger no more . . ."

He looked so sad and disappointed that I thought: What the hake. So I wiped the bench with my good handkerchief and sat beside him. The bench was still a little damp and I hoped that I wouldn't get an attack of piles.

He lapsed into his silence and started to stare again, preoccupied with his sad thoughts, and I felt I should say something to cheer him up. "We had some good times in the shop," I said. "Remember, Baptiste? Remember the day we set the time clock ahead and everybody stomped out of the shop a half-hour early and old Gus the foreman was going crazy yelling out the window to come back, that he was going to fire the whole shop? And how about those Easter sunrise mornings, eh, Baptiste? How about that?"

His face brightened. Ordinarily, I don't like to think

about those days because you can't bring them back but I began to talk about those long-ago Easter mornings and he seemed to be listening and enjoying himself, nodding his head and chuckling once in a while. There's an old Canadian legend that the sun dances on the water on the morning of the Resurrection of Our Lord. For many years, Baptiste and I and some other fellow, Ernie Saulnier or Ray Remier, would go to Moosock Brook at the far edge of town to see the miracle. We would either stay up all night celebrating the end of Lent or set our alarm clocks for four o'clock in the morning and we'd shiver our way through the gray, milky streets, stopping now and then to take long pulls at whisky to keep us warm. Sometimes it rained or was cloudy or a morning mist hid the sun but there were lots of years when the sun rose and the rays would dance on the water and we would be wild and soaring with the drink and the wonder of it all. The dawn always started pale and innocent as a child's face and then would turn crimson and gold and the whisky would build fires in me and everything would be warm and good, the way it feels when you are curled up cozy and sweet with a woman warm beside you. The sun would change to a blazing, painted woman and I'd say to myself that it was a sin to be thinking like that on a Holy Day when I should be remembering how Christ died for us on the Cross. And that would make me so remorseful that I would tug out the bottle again, drinking away my burden of sin. And the sun would send its rays leaping and skipping on the surface of the brook, dazzling pink and silver where the water flickered on the stones and rocks, and we'd be caught by the miracle and jump and sing with delight. We'd take our empty bottles down to the edge of the brook and bend over to let the water bubble inside because everyone believed that Easter water was miraculous and could cure diseases and mend broken bones. One year Baptiste fell in the brook, splashing and thrashing around wildly, laughing and singing as he stood knee-deep in the water, and he pulled me in with him. We didn't mind the wet and the cold but the dunking sobered us off and Baptiste was indignant about that. Later, we'd edge our way back to Mechanic Street, our arms flung around each other, disgracing ourselves before the proper people returning from the early Mass at St. Jude's, the women raising their eyebrows like teachers' pointers, and the men secretly jealous of us. We'd make our way to Ernie's house where his mother would slice the good, thick slabs of ham and scuttle some potatoes in the frying pan and chop up some onions to fry and we'd eat heartily, drinking big gulps of coffee, and be ready for the last Mass at church. My mother always exploded with anger at me because of the sunrise antics and she'd throw out the Easter water, and I would have to go to church every day for the next week at six in the morning, before she'd forgive me.

The memories unbent Baptiste a little and he said: "Your *maman* was one fine woman. She could cook the *tourtière*, best tam meat pie I ever taste. But she always want for me to get marry." He sniffed the air, his nostrils tasting the wind the way the farmers in Canada test the weather. "Me, I should have took her advise. A bach all your life is no good. Remember those girl at the shop what I dance with at the party all the time? I should have took one and marry her and then have one big nice *famille* and a big table surround with lots of kid . . ." He looked at me. "You was marry with Sophie for a time and that was lucky for you even though you got no kid . . ."

He sighed in a funny way and deepened in thought and

began to hum softly to himself, staring again across the street. But I realized that he wasn't looking anywhere really, and I had the feeling that if I passed my hand in front of his eyes he wouldn't blink. He stayed that way awhile, humming along, no particular tune, and then closed his eyes. He slouched down on the bench and I started to get mad. I realized he hadn't bothered to find out anything new about me, whether I was working or retired, and he stayed like that, his eyes closed and his humming going on. I would have gotten up and left but I had no place to go at the moment.

The sun was still bright and flashing on the street, and people hurried by, everybody going somewhere, women pushing along those supermarket baskets filled with groceries and young fellows and girls walking hand in hand, and little children tugging at their mothers to explain about the big monument that was all covered up. I like to watch people like that, although it depresses me most of the time. Like the pretty girls. I like to watch the pretty girls going by in their high-heel shoes and nylon stockings and gay dresses. The delicate way they hold themselves as if their beauty would break if they stepped too hard. But I begin pitying them after a while because someday they'll wake up to find that they're not young and pretty anymore, and they'll have to wear corsets and grease themselves up with cold cream at night and start being nice to people that they wouldn't even look at twice when they were young and beautiful.

But I didn't feel any better looking at the plain girls. The plain girls walk different from the pretty ones: they don't seem to be in such a hurry to get any place and they look around when they walk, at other people or things, and there's a sadness about them even when they look happy because they know that they'll never come into a room and have some fellow go crazy about them on the spot, love at first sight like in the movies with the music playing. A plain girl will probably fall in love someday and have a fellow love her back, but it doesn't happen all of a sudden like it will to a pretty girl.

Sophie was a plain girl. She wasn't plain, exactly. She was homely, if you want the truth. I met her too late, not a young man anymore, and she herself didn't have the bloom of spring in her cheeks but was forty-one years old. She worked as a driller at the shop, making those tiny holes in the barrettes, and I would stop at her bench and talk to her and joke a little. One night when I was singing with the drink at Lu's Place I called her at her rooming house and went around later and sat on the piazza with her. She wasn't pretty and she was big-boned, but she was gentle and tender and moved lightly for a woman her size and she read poetry and didn't laugh when I told her that poetry brought tears to my eyes. Work was good in the shop in those days with no layoffs, and suddenly there weren't any wild weekends, and I'd leave Lu's Place early in the evening because there was nothing to look for there anymore.

We were married on a Monday morning at the seven-o'clock Mass at St. Jude's Church with only a few friends in the pews and we took the nine-fifteen train to Boston and stayed in a hotel there for our honeymoon. I went to night school and got my diploma and I didn't mind feeling a little ridiculous: a grown man of forty-five sitting at a small desk, a married man with a wife at home expecting a baby. At the end of the term I won a medal for writing a poem and Sophie sat in the audience and began to clap when I walked across the stage and other people started to clap, too, in that scattered way when they're not sure what they're clapping about.

Sometimes I'd wake up in the night and see Sophie sleeping, her face all loose and unguarded, the childhood chickenpox marks on her cheeks, her nose too flat and big above the thin lips and her shoulders too husky. I'd almost cry because she hadn't met a fellow when she was younger and hadn't known what it was like to have somebody flirt with her across a room or dance every dance with her at St. Jean's Hall on a summer night. And nobody but me ever discovered the loveliness of her: she used to tell me how awkward and embarrassed she felt when she was a young girl waiting for someone to ask her to dance and trying to pretend that she didn't care if nobody asked her. But, in the end, she was lovely. The baby growing in her opened up the prettiness of her even though she gained too much weight and had swollen ankles and suffered from indigestion during most of her pregnancy.

I didn't want to think about Sophie anymore because sooner or later I would think of that hospital room, and I turned in anger to Baptiste. He had shut me out and had started all those sad thoughts. I could see that he wasn't asleep because his eyelids fluttered. I tried to think of something to say, to start him talking. I was getting pretty lonesome.

"Say, Baptiste," I said. "Know where I can find a job?"

After a while he opened his eyes, sighing. "Highway department. Clean street. Hire old men for summer. See foreman name of Johnson. One dollar ten cent to the hour . . ."

You had to hand it to Baptiste. He always knew things like that, jobs, and who to see and what the pay rate was. And I was happy suddenly, pleased that he at least was talking again and knew what was going on in the world. I myself had forgotten all about the highway department and how they always hired men in the spring for the roadwork and didn't mind taking on older men as long as they could push a broom or make themselves useful.

"That's great, Baptiste," I said. "I was kind of getting the blues wondering about a job. I think I'll have to check into that . . ."

"Now's good time to go," he said.

"No, I think I'll enjoy myself for a day or so and maybe drop in there day after tomorrow . . ."

He didn't say anything, only sighed, and I wondered whether he was trying to get rid of me. The silence fell again between us and the sky clouded over once more and took the shine away from everything but I was happy thinking about that job with the highway department. Silence always makes me uncomfortable. The only man I ever enjoyed silence with was Stretch because it wasn't an empty, shutting-out-people silence but a quiet, friendly thing.

"Where you living, Baptiste?" I asked. "You got a nice place?" I wasn't really interested because rooms are all the same but I felt like talking a bit.

"Nice," he said, his eyes still closed.

"Where is it?" I asked. "I've got to be finding me a place sometime, my room's too small." There I was lying again but I didn't want to mention that I didn't have any arrangements made for the night: he might start thinking I was hinting for an invitation.

He didn't answer me and I touched his arm. "Baptiste, where did you say you live? I didn't hear you."

He opened his eyes and stared at me. "What you mean by where I live?"

"I mean where you live," I said, getting a little annoyed. He was sure acting peculiar.

"What for you want to know this?" he asked, his eyes glittering and alert now as if he had *really* been asleep and had just awakened.

What the hake. I didn't know why I had asked him where he lived. "I was just making conversation, that's all," I said.

He continued to stare at me, as if I was a stranger, somebody he'd never seen before. "What business you got to know where I live?" he asked, looking suspicious, like I was a spy or a secret agent or something.

"No business," I said. "I was just talking. You know, just talking . . ."

He leaped to his feet and his eyes were narrow as he looked down at me. I was shocked by how gaunt he was, his cheeks hollow and sucked in as if he was about to whistle. His shoulders were hunched forward like he was warding off a chill. "What people send you to find out these thing?" he asked, his voice rising and his hands trembling as he pulled at his chin.

I stood up so that he wouldn't raise his voice any louder and create a scene. He wasn't as tall as in the old days, hunched over as he was. "What's the matter, Baptiste?" I asked, gentle as I could. "What are you getting sore about? I was just being friendly. We used to be good friends . . ."

He scratched his cheek in an uncertain manner, his eyes judging me in a strange way. "Leave me be," he cried in a strangled voice, backing away, a trapped look on his face.

"Baptiste," I said, "I'm Tommy Bartin, your old friend."

"I got no friend who talks," he said, tearing the words out of himself in terror. He kept backing away, clutching his jacket, as if I was carrying some kind of plague he would catch. He looked around wildly for a moment and then hurried away, brushing against people in the crowd and not slowing down to pardon himself or anything.

Well, let him go, I said to myself. He's acting crazy as a bedbug and why fool around with a crazy man? I caught sight of his figure as he weaved through the crowd, almost like a drunken man, crossing the street without watching the traffic and dodging a big truck that almost knocked him down.

I thought of the good times we'd had together and said to myself: What the hake. I can't let him run around loose like that, he'll get himself killed in an accident. And I began to follow him.

BAPTISTE LED ME a merry chase although it wasn't merry at all and it wasn't much of a chase because he didn't seem to know or care whether I or anybody else was following him.

He walked all over the business section and he didn't seem to have any destination at all. Once in a while he would stop and look into a store window and then he would glance up at the new electronic clock in the traffic circle.

I had no trouble keeping him in sight because there was a drifting way about him that set him apart from the other people who were rushing back and forth with no time to dawdle. Baptiste acted like he was the only man alive in the world. Once in a while he'd bump into somebody as he turned into the sidewalk traffic after studying the merchandise in a store window.

This sort of business went on for almost an hour and after a while I realized that he was standing in front of the various stores for five minutes and then standing at the curb for another five minutes and then moving on to a new store and repeating that time sequence. I kept my distance from him and he never suspected I was around as he visited just about every store in town, even visiting one place *twice*, the children's store, when, I figured, he got mixed up on his schedule. I thought how crazy he must be to be doing a thing like this, and I wondered how long he had been carrying on that way. Yet he didn't look crazy. Then I wondered if this was a little schedule he had made out to pass the time, something to while away the empty hours. I mean, everybody has some kind of schedule for doing things and why not a schedule for looking in store windows, if you like to look in store windows? I stood there feeling bad for him, having to fill his life with that kind of thing. Finally, when the clock on top of the monument said 1:45, he started walking with swift steps, his head down, as if he had an appointment someplace.

I followed him as he crossed the street. He seemed to be heading for the park bench but instead he continued along and stopped before a shoe store. He looked around suspiciously for the first time, as if he sensed that somebody was watching him. Then he tried to look casual, brushing lint from his jacket, but you could see him glancing around with eyes that looked shrewd, although I had to guess at this because I was across the street, watching him in a mirror in a furniture-store window. Finally, he entered a doorway next to the shoe store so quickly that it looked as if he had disappeared by magic. I waited a moment and crossed the street and went through the doorway myself. I wasn't sure what I was going to do but it was clear that he needed a friend, maybe somebody to talk to that he could trust. I knew I could convince him that I was still his friend if he gave me a chance.

The door opened onto a steep flight of steps: there was no foyer or hallway. I heard his slow, lumbering footsteps on the stairs above. I waited again and went up the stairs, a little worried about the way my chest was aching and my heart pounding. At the second-floor landing, it was clear that this was a rooming house: there were a lot of doors on both sides of the hallway and most of them were open. A radio blared music and there was something sizzling in a frying pan and the smell of hamburg spiced the air and the voice of a woman, whining and complaining. The funny part about it all was that these sounds were muted, as if there was some level of sound that the landlord had established or the people themselves had decided on, so that it was actually quiet and I had the feeling I could hear a pin drop if somebody dropped a pin.

I climbed the second flight of stairs, pausing to rest two or three times, because the stairs in this building were steeper than regular stairs. The top floor was identical to the floor below: all those doors, most of them open. I glanced into the nearest room and saw the dingy painted walls the color of chocolate that had melted and hardened again, and the old battered furniture. There was a fried smell there too, something like hamburg, and I guess that was the regular smell of the place and it gave me a lonesome feeling. People eating fried things all the time is terrible: it means they have nobody to cook a good roast for, it means they're alone.

I leaned against the banister, gathering my strength, wondering into which room Baptiste had vanished, when a woman came out of one of the doorways. It was hard to tell how old she was because her face was covered with cold cream and her hair was twisted every which way in pin curlers. She wore a shapeless, flowered housecoat that had some buttons missing and she clutched at the front of the housecoat to keep her fat stomach covered. Funny thing: she only seemed fat in the stomach and yet she was too old to be carrying a baby. She also had beautiful lips. Her face was puffy under her eyes and her eyebrows looked tweezed to death but her lips were pale pink and delicate, curving nicely, and when she spoke her voice was soft and warm.

"Were you looking for someone?" she asked in a lovely voice. She looked as if she was sixty years old but her voice was young, like a girl's. "Anyone who climbed all those stairs must be looking for someone and it must be important."

"Jean-Baptiste La Chapelle," I said, still fighting to get my wind back. "I guess he lives here somewhere . . ."

"Oh, the Canuck," she said, wrinkling her nose. She said it in a disgusted way and I should have gotten angry at her but I kept looking at her lips and enjoying that voice of hers. And I felt guilty, still liking her voice and lips after she talked like that. It was not so much the word *Canuck* but the way she said it.

"The door that's closed," she said. "Next to the bathroom." She pointed toward the far end of the hallway where there were two closed doors. I chuckled a little, thinking that she acted as if I could tell a bathroom by the door alone. I asked her which one was Baptiste's door because I would have felt foolish knocking at the door of a bathroom, especially if somebody happened to open it.

"The first door," she said, "the other one is the janitor's bathroom." She seemed annoyed, as if she'd expected me to know which room was which. "Almost everybody keeps their door open except late at night, of course, but not Mr. Frenchman. Like he's got secrets or something. Everybody likes a little company, keeping their doors open just to know that there's somebody next door moving around, but not *him*." She leaned toward me and I had to step back a little, afraid that her big stomach would touch me. "Why, do you know," she asked, whispering, "do you know nobody's ever seen the inside of his place? Living here two years and nobody, my dear, nobody, has ever peeked in that door? Acts like he's got some high and mighty treasure in there. And he hardly talks to anybody, always gruff or glaring at us, *glaring* at us, my dear. Are you a friend of his? I didn't think he had any friends . . ."

I drew further away from her, thinking how cruel people are and sorry that she had such a beautiful voice because, somehow, it stopped me from really resenting her.

Before I could answer, Baptiste stepped out of his door and went into the janitor's bathroom.

"You see?" the woman asked, as if Baptiste's appearance had proved something. "He doesn't even use his own bathroom. He pays George the janitor a dollar a month to let him use that hall bathroom. And nobody can go near the place for an hour after he's through his visit . . ."

She suddenly cocked her head to one side and listened sharply. "Oh, there's my serial. I wonder if the doctor's going to operate on Dorrie today . . ." I guess she was talking about some television program. I couldn't sort out the different sounds coming from the apartments: radios playing and somebody coughing and a high giggle and a big belch, all at that quiet pitch as if there was a giant volume control for the whole building. And the sounds were strange in another way: they were all separate sounds, they didn't sound cheerful as if they came from people all together in one room.

The woman tiptoed away, her head still cocked as if she could already hear her program, and I stood there waiting for Baptiste to appear. I decided to walk down toward his room. Suddenly he came out of the bathroom and saw me. He stood frozen for a moment, that same look of terror sweeping his face. He dashed toward his room, lunging for the knob, and I ran down to him. He was inside the room as I arrived at the door but he wasn't quick enough to shut me out and I shoved my foot inside, the way I've heard salesmen do. I could hear his breath coming in gasps and I pushed against the door. He suddenly grunted in surprise and the door swung open and I almost pitched headfirst into the room.

He was sprawled on the floor, having tripped on the edge of the linoleum, I guess, and he cried up at me: "No . . . no . . . go away . . ."

I shut the door behind me so that the other people in the building, especially that woman with the cold cream, wouldn't come running and see his apartment. If Baptiste didn't want them seeing his place, it was his privilege, and I admired him for his independence.

He remained on the floor and drew up his knees and bowed his head between them, crying, huge sobs shaking his shoulders and arms. I leaned against the door, speaking gentle words to him, words you can't recall afterward, like when you're trying to soothe a baby. He kept on crying and sobbing and I looked up at the room, and saw the dolls.

There must have been twenty dolls in the place, dolls of all shapes and sizes, girl and boy dolls and a baby doll in a small, toy bassinet, and bigger dolls that seemed old enough, if you looked quick, to be mistaken for five-year-old children. Some dolls were sitting on an old davenport and some standing at different spots in the rooms, their arms and legs in various postures. A big kitchen table, covered with one of those old-fashioned oilcloths, was neatly set as if for a big party with eight chairs arranged there, two on each side of the table. A doll sat in each chair but one, propped up on cardboard boxes or old books piled high. I guess the empty chair was for Baptiste himself. I rubbed my eyes: it was as if I had been watching a motion picture all day and when I came into this room the movie stopped, the action frozen the way it happens sometimes in a theater.

He lifted his head and looked at me pitifully. "What for you come here?" he asked, calmer now, but his rough old face damp with tears. "Now you see—what for you come?" He began to rock himself slowly on the floor, back and forth.

A sickness spread in my stomach.

"This my home," Baptiste said, "my *famille,* my nice little kid. I care for them and we talk and have one fine time together."

"Baptiste, Baptiste," I whispered, feeling tears spring to my own eyes, for some reason.

"They send you, all the other peoples here, to find out what I got in this place. To find my *famille* and take them away . . ."

I tore my eyes away from the dolls, those terrible vacant faces. The air was heavy and close, a museum smell hanging over everything.

Without warning, Baptiste leaped to his feet, his eyes lighted with frenzy. He grabbed one of the dolls from the davenport, a doll about three feet high dressed in a Scottish kilt. He clutched the doll to his chest. "What for you do this?" he shouted. "Can't a man make himself private? I bother nobody, mind my own affair but no one leave me be, always someone spy, stare at me, follow me sometime . . ."

"It's not right, Baptiste," I said, gasping for air, wanting to fling the door open and let in a fresh breeze.

"Shut your face," he bellowed, clinging to that doll for all he was worth.

His entire body began to tremble and he took two or three steps backward and fell, sitting, to the davenport. The tears rolled down his cheeks.

I only wanted to get out of there: I was afraid that any moment I would see the dolls begin to move or hear them speak and I knew I would drop dead right in front of them. But I didn't want to leave him like that and at least he was sitting down now and didn't look so wild.

"Look, Baptiste," I said, gentle as I could. "It's all right to have dolls around like this but you should have other friends, too. Real ones. Like the people here in the building. They're all nice people, just like yourself. Lonesome, wanting to be friendly if you give them a chance . . ." My voice didn't sound very convincing to me: it reminded me of the way the nurses used to talk at the hospital.

"What you know about lonesome?" he said, getting riled up again, his voice rising. "With my *famille* I not lonesome so much no more. But everybody want to take them away. They send you, everybody jealous about Baptiste and his friends, and they want to take my *famille* away . . ." He leaped to his feet again, still clutching that doll. "But no one take them away, no one . . . I won't let them take away . . ." He took a step or two toward me and an awful dizziness swept my head. "You going to tell them, you tell them and they come here and take them away . . ."

I fell back against the door to steady myself and heard myself saying: "Nobody sent me here, Baptiste, and, anyway, why should I tell anybody, if this is what you want? Everybody's got different things they like. To tell you the truth, I always kind of liked dolls myself. Sophie and me, we had two or three dolls around the place when we were married . . ." Keep talking, I urged myself, hoping he wouldn't come any closer because his eyes had a wild look now. "If it makes you happy, that's all right with me, Baptiste. I was just worried about you, that's all, because you looked like you lost a lot of weight and I was going to invite you out for a bite to eat with me . . ."

He blinked and shuddered and looked uncertain. "You tell no one?" he asked.

"Baptiste," I said, making my voice sound reasonable. "Who would I tell? I've been out of town for years and I'm leaving town tonight . . ."

He looked at me suspiciously. "You ask about getting job this after' . . ." he said.

That surprised me, his remembering that. It goes to show you that a man may be crazy but he isn't necessarily dumb. I said: "After I left you today, I met an old friend and he offered me a job in Boston and that's why I was going to invite you out to eat, to kind of celebrate . . ."

He sniffed a few times, the way a child does when the tears are drying and the lights are on in the bedroom again after a bad dream. I wondered how I could get out of there with no more of this crazy conversation.

He sighed and set down the Scotch doll on the davenport. With my right hand I groped for the doorknob behind me.

"You want to meet my *famille*?" he asked. "They all nice kid. I introduce you with them and all you got do is make pretend a little . . ."

"Gee, Baptiste," I said, my hand finding the doorknob, "I'd really like to meet them because I always kind of liked dolls myself. But like I said I've got to leave town tonight and I wanted to do a little shopping . . ."

"You ask me out to eat with you," he said, his face getting crafty suddenly.

"Yes, sure, but I figured I'd meet you later unless you want to tramp around all those stores with me." I was turning the doorknob slowly, knowing I had to get out of there in one piece and call a doctor or a policeman or somebody to help him.

A slyness glittered in his eyes. "You fool Baptiste? You try to fool Baptiste? You want to go to bring back the peoples and take my *famille* away . . ." He took a couple of steps toward me.

I yanked the door open and we stood looking at each other for one terrible moment, his eyes wild and unbelieving and yet a kind of belief in them at the same time, as if he had known all the time that this was going to happen. I whirled around and stepped into the hallway and he bounded toward the door.

There were two or three women in the hallway, looking at us, the woman with the cold cream on her face among them. "You lie," Baptiste yelled, hurtling toward me. But he noticed the women and you could see the sudden terror in his eyes, and the indecision. He didn't know whether to chase me or get back in that apartment and close his door before they saw the dolls.

He lunged back into the room, slamming the door and yelling: "Don't tell, Tommy, don't tell peoples . . ."

I didn't stay around there. I brushed past the women, their eyes and mouths gaping at me like fish in an aquarium, and I ran down the stairs.

SOMETIMES you can't get drunk. You can swallow all the beer and wine and whisky in the world and get dizzy and giddy and lose your balance when you leave the bar stool and lurch to the men's room but a small dark place inside of you stays untouched and dry and cold. I haunted the bars and saloons after Sophie died, drinking steady, staying out of work although it was the rush season at the shop. I avoided my friends, visiting the uptown bars away from Mechanic Street, where I figured nobody would see me and try to talk some sense into me.

But finally I stopped drinking and went back to the shop because I never got drunk and the liquor only honed the pain.

That was the feeling I had as I hunched over the bar at a place called the Harbor Arms at the end of Main Street on the other side of the square. Two shots of whisky and three glasses of beer had left me feeling numb and empty and that was all, and the memory of Baptiste in his room full of dolls still gave me the chills. I wondered whether I had been right or wrong. Standing downstairs at his building, I had decided against calling the police or a doctor, figuring that he wasn't hurting anybody, really, and that everybody is a little peculiar at times.

The bartender, one of those professional kind wearing a neat white shirt and a black tie and a little maroon vest with brass buttons, looked at me strangely, his eyes narrowing, and I wondered whether I'd talked aloud to myself. I signaled for another glass of beer.

The Harbor Arms was a fancy place, soft lights, the bulbs hidden behind the woodwork at the edge of the ceiling. In a place like that you need the lights on even in the middle of the day. The nearest harbor was fifty miles away in Boston but a big mural on the wall facing the bar showed a scene filled with fishing boats and wharves and sea gulls flying. I realized I looked out of place in a bar like that, an older man drinking boilermakers, but I wasn't caring too much about appearances at the moment. I wondered whether I *should* call somebody to help Baptiste. But how would they help him? Maybe take him away for treatments or lock him up?

A middle-aged fellow who looked like one of those business executives sat at the end of the bar, a leather briefcase on the counter near his glass. He was drinking something fancy in a tall, long-stemmed glass. "Tommy," he called, "is Tootsie going to show up tonight? She sobered up yet?"

I was glad to hear somebody call my name and was about to tell him that he'd made a mistake, that I didn't know anybody by the name of Tootsie but that I'd be glad to make a little conversation, when the bartender spoke up. His name was Tommy, too, I guess.

"She'd better," he said. "She's drying out right now over at the motel . . ." The bartender looked annoyed. He shouldn't have looked annoyed. A real professional bartender should never let his feelings show. Lu had told me that.

The executive fellow left his stool and walked over to a placard standing on an easel at the far end of the place. The placard showed a few pictures of a girl in different poses with hardly any clothes on. Although the light was dim, I could read the big lettering at the top: "ALL THIS WEEK—TOOTSIE ROLLE." I figured that name wasn't her own.

"Man, what a pair," the fellow said, standing and admiring the placard. "I never saw such a pair on a girl . . ." He was shaking his head. "A lush but luscious . . ."

There was an open door near the placard and I could see a small stage at the end of the next room, looking lonesome the way empty stages always do. The executive fellow was still shaking his head in admiration and I thought how fellows in bars were all the same whether it was a fancy bar with soft lights or a neighborhood saloon like Lu's Place.

I was wondering whether I should tell the bartender my name was Tommy like his and I decided suddenly that maybe I should do something about Baptiste. Maybe he would run wild and berserk and hurt somebody.

I felt a pressure inside me and looked around for the men's room, spotting it down near the placard. I finished my beer and stepped off the stool and fell flat on my face, my legs giving way and my knees buckling and my cheek hitting the floor. I hoped I was hurt, in a way, so that I could stay there awhile and not get up and face the bartender and the executive fellow, and I was thankful there was nobody else around. I struggled to my feet, dizzy, but I was suddenly happy and I heard myself giggle. Yes sirree, I thought, I'm drunk all right. I stood up and was glad the fellows didn't come to help me although both of them were watching me closely, the executive forgetting all about Miss Tootsie Rolle and the bartender looking at me in a funny way. I didn't blame him. I mean, it's kind of funny when you stop to think about it, when a fellow suddenly falls flat on his face. It happens all the time in the movies and everybody laughs. I tried to smile at them to assure them that I wasn't hurt.

"Gentlemen," I said, bowing my head, showing that a man could keep his dignity after falling on the floor, and I walked out of there, glad that I didn't have to go to the bathroom after all.

I stood outside the place for a minute, getting my balance, thinking that I should eat something but my appetite was gone. After a while, the dizziness went away and only a pleasant glow remained.

I walked toward that electric clock on top of the crazy monument and it said: 2:16. I let the people drift by me, going in and out of stores, and wondered whether I should buy some new clothes now and join in with the holiday shoppers or wait awhile. It was nice trying to make up my mind: I hadn't had any decisions like that to make for a long time. Then I decided to wait until after Memorial Day because I didn't want to be loaded down with a lot of packages.

As I neared the Common, a half-ton truck pulled up at the curb and parked near a fire hydrant although there were spaces open at the parking meters. The power of politics, I guess, because the truck had a seal on the door that said: "City of Monument—Park Department." Two big geezers got out and started to carry flags and bunting and other paraphernalia over to the platform at the bottom of the veiled monument. I hiccuped and missed my footing as I stepped off the curb. I *did* feel a little drunk although I was actually under control and it was a pleasant, tipsy feeling to tell the truth.

From the Common, I could see the apartment building where Baptiste lived. I was afraid to look over there, afraid that I would see something terrible—I hated to think of what

I would see—but I finally looked, trying to figure out which room was his but my eyes got blurry when I strained them, squinting. Anyway, the building seemed calm enough and Baptiste wasn't looking out a window or yelling his head off or anything. I thought: Poor fellow, why not let him alone, why not let him enjoy himself with his dolls?

The geezers were starting to decorate the platform, draping the bunting around the four sides of the railings and on the ladder that led up to the base of the statue. A few people stopped to watch the work and it felt nice standing there in the crowd, curious about the monument and what it would turn out to be when some official or other climbed the ladder and pulled away the canvas. I thought of all the other Memorial Days and how the band and the soldiers always visited the cemeteries in town. They marched to the French and Irish cemeteries which were not too far from the square. Then the buses took them to the Protestant cemetery beyond Norton's Pond on the hill and from there they marched back to the center of town and stood at attention in the square. A smart kid from the high school would get up on the platform and recite the Gettysburg Address by heart and the mayor would welcome everybody and give a speech and one of the Legion officers would then introduce the main speaker, maybe a senator or an army general. The main speaker always talked on and on and almost spoiled the whole affair, and if it was a hot day, two or three of the paraders would pass out. At the end of the ceremonies, a firing squad would raise their rifles and let off a volley and one bugler would stand in the Common to blow Taps while another bugler stood at the far end of the square, echoing the long sad sounds and it almost made you feel like crying.

The geezers were doing a terrible job of putting up the

banners and the bunting, letting the material sag too far down. I turned away because slipshod workmanship always riles me. There suddenly seemed no place to go, and I decided to find a bed to sleep in that night. There were some rooming houses near the library on West Street a short distance from the Common, across from the Elks Hall and the American Legion headquarters. I figured I would find a place to rent and then freshen up and come back downtown, have a big meal someplace and then buy a newspaper and find out all about the main speakers and the time of the parade tomorrow morning and then go to the movies. It felt good making plans like that.

Across from the square, I saw a liquor store and went inside to stock up. I counted my pockets: four in my pants and three in my jacket, and I asked the clerk for seven of those little nip bottles that sell for forty-five cents each. That was an old trick of mine. I never liked to carry around pints of whisky because you had to duck into an alley for a drink when you felt thirsty for one. But these little nips were different. There were a couple of good gulps in each and I'd place a bottle in each pocket and slip one out, hiding it with my hand, and could take a drink any time. Of course, I only did that on special occasions, at a parade or going to a foot-ball game. The clerk, a snappy-looking fellow, wearing a red bow tie, with a pink baby face but not a wisp of hair on his head, tried to talk me into buying one big bottle. I insisted on the nips although it was more expensive that way. I told him to never mind a bag and I placed them in my pockets. "Neat trick, eh?" I asked. He didn't seem impressed and turned away without saying anything.

Up the street I passed the library and almost stopped in. The reading room was a favorite place of mine, all the newspapers hanging from wooden rods like curtains, the *New York Times* and the *Wall Street Journal,* although I seldom read those newspapers because they didn't have enough pictures and the stories were too long. Sometimes I'd pick one up and start reading it and it felt good when somebody came in and saw me and probably thought I was an executive of some big company checking on the stock market. I didn't stop in at the library though because the sky was darkening again and there was a distant rumble of thunder and I wanted to get settled in a room.

I stopped in front of an old tall thin house that looked as neat and proper as an old lady all corseted up. There was a sign in a window saying: "ROOMS TO LET." I rang the bell but it didn't work, so I knocked on the frosted window that had some fancy curlicues in the glass. A little old woman, so short that a tall fellow might trip over her if he didn't see her coming, opened the door. She was all sharp edges: her cheekbones, her thin shoulders under a crocheted purple shawl, her nose and chin. She glared at me as if I was a criminal.

"I see you've got a room to rent, madam," I said, making my voice sound like a college professor. "I would like to apply for it . . ."

She sniffed, her nose wrinkling and her eyes glittering. "You smell like a brewery," she said, the words sharp as scissors cutting cloth.

"Pardon the odor, madam," I said. "I had a brief fainting spell downtown from the heat and a man forced me to take a sip or two of some awful stuff, brandy or whisky or something. I'm glad that none of my friends were there or I would have been disgraced."

"You didn't get that smell from one sip of whisky," she

said. "You smell like you were born in a saloon and didn't leave it until today . . ."

She slammed the door in my face, rattling the window. I went down the steps and sat on the small cement wall at the edge of the sidewalk, annoyed that I hadn't bothered to buy any Sen Sen for my breath. I sat there awhile, looking across at the Elks Hall, a big, ancient house that used to be owned by one of the old-time families of the town. I had a feeling someone was looking at me and I glanced toward the house just in time to see a curtain moving near a window. The old woman must have been watching me and I told myself to get out of that vicinity quick, because she looked like the kind that would call the police and have a man arrested.

I stood up and started back down toward town. It seemed that the best thing to do was to hire one of the terrible rooms in the Rainbow Hotel, a cheap place above the Rainbow Bar at the edge of the business section where the railroad tracks passed by close enough to shake the tenements. It was the section of town people called Junkville that the city kept saying it was going to tear down but never did. I figured I could hire a room in the hotel for a couple of nights and then get a job and buy some decent clothes and move to a respectable neighborhood.

As I walked along I noticed all these old people across the street heading toward the Elks Hall. They were dressed up as if it was Sunday afternoon and I counted twenty-two people either walking or already climbing up the steps, and there wasn't a young person anywhere in sight, just these old men and women. It reminded me of one of those science-fiction programs on the television where something weird happens to the world: like everybody suddenly turning into old people. Then I remembered that the Happy Timers held their meetings in the Elks Hall and Charlie Morrissey had mentioned that a big meeting was going to be held the afternoon before he got married, when the club was planning a party for his bride-to-be and him.

I was tempted to follow along with the old people and join in the meeting just as Charlie had invited me to do. But to tell the truth, the sight of so many walking along and going up the steps discouraged me. Still, they were all stepping smartly, calling to each other and joking with each other. Most of the women carried packages that looked like homemade cakes: you know those brown square boxes people carry cakes in?

A clap of thunder shook the sky and a few raindrops began to fall and I thought: What the hake, I might as well go to that meeting and get out of the rain.

As I crossed the street, I saw an old fellow struggling up the steps, stopping on each step to rest. A little old lady came along, stepping fast like a busy rabbit, and she helped him up the stairs, holding his arm. That must be terrible, having an old lady like that help you up the stairs.

That almost stopped me from going to the meeting. But I had my nips in my pocket and it was raining anyway and it seemed like the proper thing to do, to pay my respects to Charlie and his girl friend.

"THE MEETING will come to order," the fellow called Long John said as he stood at the microphone on the small stage at the far end of the hall. Long John was pretty deaf and he'd forgotten his hearing aid that day, and he had a sickly wife by the name of Matilda that he cared for like a baby and he always stood too near the microphone so that most of the people didn't know what he was talking about half the time.

I found out all this stuff about Long John because I had a seat, in the last row, directly behind two women who kept up a steady stream of chatter. Most of the Happy Timers sat near the stage, but those two women in front of me—one named Martha and the other Emma—took seats down at the back and I discovered the reason soon enough: they'd rather talk than listen, and being so far in the rear they could talk to their hearts' content and nobody would complain.

It was lucky for me they sat there because they hid me from the rest of the people in the hall (they were both pretty hefty women, wearing large picture hats) and there was nobody in the last row but me. That way, I could quietly sip my nips and watch the meeting, invisible to everybody.

To tell the truth, I almost didn't stay for the meeting itself. Once I got inside the Elks Hall, I found a little alcove near the door that led to the meeting hall and I stationed myself there, watching the people enter, nobody taking any notice of me. I enjoyed watching them all arrive but after a while it reminded me too much of The Place, all those old-timers under one roof. Still, they were cheerful enough, chatting and joking, and if most of them complained about their aches and pains (everybody seemed to be having trouble with their legs that day), at least they didn't moan about them but just seemed to be stating the facts of life and accepting them. There were more women than men, as you'd expect, and the women wore silk flowered dresses and had blue hair and glasses, and whether they were short or tall or fat or skinny, they all kind of looked alike. A lot of them carried glass-handled umbrellas. The men didn't carry umbrellas and I'll say one thing for them: they were dressed up dandy, most of them, in sports coats and nice colored sports shirts and it pleased me to be seeing them wearing clothes like that because I myself believe in colorful clothes and my green-plaid jacket is the most cheerful thing I ever bought.

I got restless after a while. There was a woman standing at the entrance of the hall, sort of an official greeter, who kissed all the ladies on the cheek as they entered, and she kept glancing at me in a suspicious way. I was dying for a drink but I hated to take a chance, knowing how the Happy Timers didn't approve of drinking. My stomach felt empty and weak and I was annoyed at myself for not eating practically anything all day long.

The official-greeter woman finally left her post and I took advantage of the situation to peek into the meeting hall. I didn't want Charlie to make a fuss over me and decided I would just go up later and shake his hand and maybe have a piece of cake and then leave. The hall was long and narrow with a stage at the far end and a microphone at the front of the stage. A big sign hung from the top of the stage. "CONGRATULATIONS, GLADYS AND CHARLIE," it said. Pink and blue ribbons were draped here and there in the hall.

Charlie stood chatting at the bottom of the stage with a huge woman in a purple dress. The woman was all bosom, from her neck to her stomach, and Charlie was looking up into her face and nodding like a henpecked husband, and I hoped that *she* wasn't Gladys. Charlie looked fine, though, all spruced up as usual, with a white carnation in his lapel. Then a little sweet-looking lady in a fancy blue dress that had a big gardenia corsage approached Charlie. She walked dainty, looking shy and embarrassed by all the fuss, and Charlie looked at her and smiled, the kind of smile I remembered from the times we'd gotten pleasantly drunk together and Charlie had leaned against a telephone pole, staring off into space in some beer dream. I felt sorry that he'd given up drinking. Anyway, she was a good-looking lady, that Gladys, and she put her hand on Charlie's arm and somehow that seemed such a nice loving gesture: just that, placing her hand on his arm. The woman with the big bosom beamed down on them and then turned away, all business, calling for everybody to "hurry up, hurry up."

By now the sight of so many oldsters gathered together in one room was making my flesh creep. I slipped into a corner in the back of the hall, behind some piled-up folded chairs, and took a drink from one of the nips, hiding it in my hand.

The old fellow, who I later learned was Long John, went to the microphone. The microphone began to screech and howl and he adjusted it and called out: "Come on, let's get this meeting going." The woman at the door pushed everybody inside and closed the door and I was trapped, all by myself in the corner. That's when good old Martha and Emma took their seats in the back of the place, and the meeting started.

Long John said: "We will observe a moment of silence for our departed members." Everybody stood up and bowed their heads and a silence fell after the chair scraping stopped and I walked softly to the empty last row and stood there like the others. This was one of the longest moments of silence I ever heard. It went on and on. Suddenly I heard a small noise: a stomach growling, the tiny curling sound a stomach makes, and it was the one called Emma right in front of me. Martha looked at her and sniffed, sort of impatient, but I felt bad for that poor Emma. I mean, what can anybody do when their stomach starts to talk like that? The silence showed no signs of letting up and I peeked around, wondering if I was missing something, and I realized that everyone in the place probably had a lot of loved ones to remember and pray for and I flushed with guilt and began to say a prayer for Sophie. Before I finished, Long John bellowed into the microphone: "We will now make the pledge of allegiance to the flag . . ." After the pledge we all sat down and I had another quick little drink.

Some of the men and women in the audience began to call to Long John, waving their hands and *psst, psst*ing him, and Martha shook her head: "Poor John," she said. "He forgot to have us sing the theme song, Emma . . ."

"And did you notice, Martha, that he's forgot his hearing aid again?" the other one answered. (That's how I learned their names: I never saw two women so in love with each other's names; they used them nearly every time they made a remark.)

Long John up there on the platform must have been a

little blind as well as deaf because he didn't pay any attention to the people waving and calling. He said: "We're going to waive the reading of the secretary's report so we can have a short meeting and get down to the business of giving Charlie and Gladys a nice party. Everybody agree?"

Well, everybody agreed excpet one fellow up in the first row who wanted to know how much money was taken in at the last whist party. He said he had charge of the refreshments for the trip they were planning in June to the Museum of Science in Boston and the treasury was getting pretty low.

"Leave it to James Howard," Martha said. "A worry-wart."

"Still, I like refreshments," Emma said, "and I like to see that there's enough to go around. Refreshments are sometimes the best thing about a trip, Martha . . ."

"There's more to life than refreshments, Emma," Martha replied.

The result of all this was that a woman by the name of Hazel Danton got up to read off how much money was taken in at the last whist party—four twenty-five—and I guess she was pretty deaf, too, because she went right on reading the entire treasurer's report right down to the last penny despite everybody hollering at her that they'd heard enough. She finished with a satisfied smile on her face and Long John looked at her kind of disgusted and shook his head.

"Now, any other business?" he asked.

Well, another woman got up from the audience and both Martha and Emma looked at each other with smirks on their faces. "Leave it to Ethel," Martha said. "She's got to make a speech at every meeting . . ."

"Thank goodness she wasn't elected president last year, Martha," Emma said.

I figured that if that Ethel was the type to make a speech I'd better take another sip and I was almost caught by the woman stationed at the door who looked in my direction just as I lowered the bottle.

It turned out that Ethel didn't want to make a speech, after all, but she thought it would be nice to hear the report of the committee for the sick. "After all," she said, "It'd be nice to hear who's in the hospital and how things are at the nursing homes." She looked around for support. "I think we ought to hear Minnie Powers' report . . ."

Well, Minnie Powers turned out to be that big bosomy woman in the purple dress. Without waiting for a vote, she marched right up there to the stage, carrying a large notebook. Long John glanced over at Charlie and Gladys, who were sitting apart from the others below the stage, and he sighed. Minnie stood at the microphone, adjusting it and fooling around as if she was going to deliver the Declaration of Independence. She began to read from the book and her voice was as powerful as her bosom but still kind of pleasant, in a way. She kept looking up to add her little comments and the people seemed to enjoy them.

Well, that sick committee certainly put in a lot of time at the job. They'd visited just about every nursing home in the city plus the hospital and Minnie said that everybody was delighted, just delighted, to see them. She went on about how poor Rose Flanagan broke her *other* hip and how John Fox was still losing weight and couldn't abide the food at the hospital and how Jessie Smith, poor thing, had another operation coming up and how Walter Crane had all the doctors baffled and how Henry Lussiere had his right leg amputated above the knee because of his diabetes, and how Josephine Carter had turned yellow with the jaundice but how everyone had been delighted to see the sick committee and had sent back their best wishes and hoped everybody would send them cards.

The list went on and on, the most depressing speech I ever heard, and it seemed like the Happy Timers had more sick members than well ones. I had time to drink one whole nip and finish half of another before she finally snapped the notebook shut and stood there looking at everybody, as if she was daring them to criticize her report. They didn't criticize at all but gave her a big round of applause and suddenly everybody seemed happier and more at ease. I wondered if it was because they'd heard about so many being sick and they were lucky enough to be here. I got kind of fuzzy at this point because the whisky was starting to make me dizzy again and I wished that the meeting would end so that I could sneak a piece of cake or maybe a sandwich.

Long John went to the microphone and then Martha herself, right in front of me, jumped to her feet and said that John had forgotten to have them sing the theme song and they shouldn't end the meeting without lifting their voices in song together, as she put it. Well, it took Long John about five minutes to get the message because of his deafness but people kept relaying it up toward the front until he finally threw up his hands and said, in his dry way: "All right. Let's have Bertha at the piano . . ."

Minnie got up again and said: "Bertha's laid up today with her arthritis, her fingers all bent, and asked me to fill in for her . . ." Minnie stomped to the piano and I was interested to see if she could fit herself to the keyboard with that big bosom of hers. The piano was out of sight but she must have made it because she struck a few chords and they sounded fine.

I told myself I was going to get out of there right away, as soon as the people stood up to sing. Cake or no cake. I thought of all these old people gathered together, half of them deaf, and all those members sick in the hospital, and the thought of them all singing together in their shaky voices was too much to bear. But suddenly, Long John was up there, leading the song and everybody was standing.

I began to edge toward the door. It was a nice tune, really, with special words sung to the melody of the "Battle Hymn of the Republic," which was always one of my favorites. I caught a few of the words and they went something like this, although I don't remember them exactly and didn't think about writing them down in my little black book:

> "When good friends get together,
> They have a lot of fun . . .
> When good friends get together,
> Etc. . . ."

Maybe it was just the music or all that whisky inside me or just that I was getting tired and feeling blue about having no place to stay yet that night and poor Baptiste up in his room alone or the fact that I didn't have a job . . . anyway, all of a sudden I felt kind of warm and my eyes got wet. The voices weren't shaky at all as they sang and everybody was swaying a little although I wasn't too sure whether it was the nips making everybody look like they were swaying.

I stood at the door and didn't feel like leaving and I realized that Charlie was right after all: it *was* a good place to go and all the people seemed happy together. I'd been sitting there sipping the whisky and sort of poking fun at them in my mind but at least they were enjoying themselves and having a good time.

They swung into another chorus of that song, the voices getting stronger and richer all the time, and Martha and Emma joined their hands and two fellows near the wall tilted their heads toward each other, sounding each other's harmony, and the voices were sweet and lovely and I was the only one in the room not singing and I wished I knew the words or could carry a tune.

> "When good friends get together
> They have a lot of fun . . ."

Long John was swinging his arms like a drum major, and the song lifted and swelled and in a pause for breath a high giggle floated on the air, a happy joy-caught giggle, and I thought how nice it was for them to have a sick committee, after all. I was starting to wish for the song to be over, though, because I was pretty dizzy and I'd decided to stay and have some cake and give my congratulations to Charlie and his Gladys.

The song ended on a high note that broke off sharply because I guess everybody was getting a little winded and then they settled back in their chairs, the women fanning themselves and the men shaking their heads as if they'd just had a good meal. I mean, everybody seemed *satisfied*.

Suddenly Charlie walked out in front of the audience and jumped to the stage in that quick, nimble way of his and whispered something in Long John's ear. John looked befuddled and Charlie tried his other ear and after a couple of minutes the message got across.

Charlie took over the microphone and shaded his eyes

with his hand and looked in my direction. He waved at me and I squirmed in my seat and there was nobody in front of me because I had moved from behind Martha and Emma during the song. I hadn't wanted him to spot me before I had a chance to tell him that I'd dropped in only to wish him well. I didn't want him to think I was going to join the club or anything, nice as that singing was.

"Ladies and gentlemen," Charlie said over the microphone, "this is a great day for Charlie Morrissey, all of you giving Gladys and me a party. But now the best thing that could've happened has happened: a dear old friend of mine is sitting in the audience . . ."

Everybody looked round, curious to see who he meant, and I shook my head frantically at Charlie, hoping he wouldn't make me stand up and take a bow, the way they do at meetings, because I was really a little drunk and the lights in the place had fuzzy halos around them.

"There he is, ladies and gentlemen, down in the back row, too shy a man to push himself forward. My old friend, Mr. Thomas Bartin . . ."

My face flushed hot as everybody turned and looked at me, and there was a little polite applause.

Charlie lifted his hands as if he was a prophet or something because he always had a tendency to show off a bit. "Now, my old friend Thomas, who everybody calls Tommy, is quite a man, ladies and gentlemen. He's a writer sort of, and he writes down a lot of wise remarks in a notebook . . . and I wouldn't be surprised if we encouraged him a little that he might come up here and favor us with one or two . . ."

I stood up so that Charlie could see more clearly as I shook my head, trying to discourage him from asking me up to the stage. I could feel the people staring at me, craning their necks and buzzing among themselves, their faces blurred.

"What say, Tommy? How about stepping down here and giving us a few words of wisdom?" Charlie called. He could be fancy when he wanted to be, and I kept shaking my head and waving my arms.

"How about some applause, ladies and gentlemen?" he asked. "He has a lot of good ideas about the world, but as you can see, he's a bashful sort and very modest . . ."

The last place in the world I wanted to go was up on that stage before all those people, especially with my head whirling and my stomach swimming and my knees weak and trembling.

The applause gathered in strength, out of politeness to Charlie, I guess, because why should a bunch of people waiting for a party to start want to hear a stranger speak to them?

Charlie started walking down the aisle toward me after leaping off the stage in that spry, healthy way that I hated about him. He reached me, grinning and shaking his head happily, and started to pull me up the aisle. The clapping got louder and I let myself be led because, to tell the truth, I was afraid I'd fall down if he let go.

Somebody had rolled a set of portable stairs to the stage by the time we got there, and Charlie led me up and turned me around to face the audience and whispered to me: "I'm glad you came, Tommy. Now read us some of those things in the book and mix in a few of the jokes . . ."

He left me standing there with that microphone in front of me. He hopped down, ignoring the steps, and settled himself beside Gladys, looking happy and pleased with himself.

I stared down into that hall full of faces and blinked my

eyes to stop the dizziness. Maybe it was the surprise of Charlie pulling me to the stage that way and the suddenness of the entire situation but, anyway, the hall stopped swaying and the blur left my eyes and I felt steadier on my feet although I clutched that microphone for all I was worth. All those faces . . . but they were looking up at me in an interested way, anticipation in their eyes, and a few of them smiled as if to give me some encouragement and suddenly I wanted to say something to them that would be fine and beautiful. I groped in my pocket for my black book and pulled it out and they started to clap again.

I leafed through the pages looking for something appropriate. The poem about the old teetotaler who broke his leg when he tripped on a drunkard's whisky keg didn't seem right. I flipped the page to that fine poem about springtime. It was a long poem but quite funny, part of it original with me and part of it taken from bits and pieces of other poems.

I cleared my throat.

"Ladies and genmulmen," I said. I'd never pronounced "gentlemen" like that before and I tried it a couple of more times to get it right. Somebody coughed and a few chairs scraped the floor. I smiled down at them, letting them think that I was just fooling around to amuse them.

"Ladies and gentle-men," I said, pinning down the word at last, smiling again with all the confidence I could muster. Nobody smiled back.

"I've got a poem here about spring." I cleared my throat again, and got started.

> "If the spring comes,
> The mattress can't be far behind . . ."

I looked down to get their reaction but most of the faces were blank and I saw Martha and Emma whispering together. My mind went as blank as the faces before me and I looked again at my book to pick up the rest of the poem although I had a feeling nobody would appreciate it. I mean, that was the best line in it, that spring-and-mattress joke, and if nobody laughed at that, they wouldn't be apt to laugh at the rest of the poem. I squinted at the page and my dizziness returned, and the words all ran together as if rain had fallen on the page. I closed the book and figured I had better recite something from memory. I glanced at Charlie, and he appeared doubtful now; there was a sickly smile on his face. The hall was quiet again, filled with a waiting silence.

"Ladies and gentle-men," I said again, being careful to pronounce the words just so. "Why do I cry?" That was my favorite comic poem that never fails to get a laugh, the one about the unbuttoned fly. I happened to glance at Gladys, sitting sweetly beside Charlie, and knew I couldn't recite that here and disgrace Charlie in front of everybody.

I let my voice drift off, trying to think of another ending. I started over again, to get my bearings.

"Ladies and gentle-men,
Why do I cry?"

I couldn't think of anything to say. People started to cough all over the place, making restless noises, and I looked down at Charlie and his face was tight with anger, his lips pressed together in straight lines.

"Why do I cry?"

I thought of something and it wasn't much but at least it would be an ending.

"I forgot to knot my tie . . ."

People looked at each other with puzzled expressions on their faces and I couldn't blame them, really. My eyes filled with water and I put my hand in my pocket to get my handkerchief. I tugged at the handkerchief and a nip bottle tumbled out and fell to the floor. It was a full one, by the sound of it. The sound wasn't so awfully loud but it was firm; in the quiet it seemed like a gavel being banged and everybody sort of came to attention and then the silence settled in again. The bottle didn't break but it began to roll and roll. We were all watching it, everybody in the hall looking at that little bottle as it turned over and over, heading toward the edge of the stage. I stood there and watched it, too, because it seemed kind of foolish to go chasing a whisky bottle in front of all those people. The bottle reached the edge of the stage and teetered there for a long moment. It was kind of terrible, everybody focused on that crazy bottle balanced on the lip of the stage and the hall so quiet that you could hear the hum from the microphone. Then the bottle fell to the floor and I heard it smash.

"Ladies and gentlemen," I began, to get their minds off the bottle. I closed my eyes to think, but not only to think. I wanted to wipe away all those faces. I began to sweat and seemed to be swimming in the darkness and there was a lot of commotion going on and I felt a tug on my arm and opened my eyes. Charlie was standing there, his eyes snapping with anger.

"Why'd you have to come and spoil everything?" he said, shaking his head in disgust.

I guess Minnie Powers was at the piano because the theme song filled the air. People were getting up from the chairs and murmuring among themselves. I wanted to apologize to Charlie, to all of them, but his face was blurred and I wasn't feeling too well physically, to tell the truth.

"I'm sorry, Charlie," I managed to say, but he didn't seem too interested.

"Why don't you just leave, Tommy?" he said. He was standing close to the microphone and it picked up his words and sent them loudly through the hall. I looked around in embarrassment but everybody seemed to be avoiding my eyes and I was just as glad. I walked off the stage and almost lost my balance going down those portable steps. People cleared a path for me and I kept my eyes straight ahead. A little old lady brandishing an umbrella headed my way. I was afraid she was going to hit me with the umbrella and I hurried my steps.

"We don't hold with whisky in the Happy Timers," she said loudly, as if it would be news to me. She halted a few feet from me, as if she didn't want to get too close, acting like I was some kind of specimen to keep away from.

Well, I didn't blame her. I got out of there fast, leaving the room in confusion behind me, the piano playing the "Battle Hymn of the Republic," and I ran waveringly down the hallway toward the outside door, hoping I wouldn't trip or fall down and make a bigger mess of everything.

I WANTED TO HIDE somewhere. The public library was back down the street, with those silent, dim-lighted stacks in the basement. The stacks were a good place to be, quiet and away from everything, so I crossed the street and walked along as steadily as I could. I looked for a place to throw my empty nip bottles because they weighed me down now, even though they were empty, but I didn't see any place that was proper to toss them.

The library was practically deserted except for a woman standing at the circulation desk, sorting some cards, and she didn't look up when I entered although I was jiggling all over the place: I had two or three empty nips in one jacket pocket and you could hear them tinkling. I thought of that little nip falling to the floor in front of all those Happy Timers and didn't think I would ever buy another.

The stacks had some stools to step on if you wanted to reach a book on a high shelf but they were also fine if you felt like sitting down. It was quiet downstairs, the old white globes on the ceiling giving off a subdued pale light. I reached up and took a book at random in the last stack at the rear of the building and sat down on a stool, leaning my back against the wall. I turned the pages and found that an old trick of mine was still in working order: looking at a book and not really reading the words and keeping my mind blank so that I wouldn't think about the Happy Timers. The title of the book was *Synonyms and Antonyms,* and to tell the truth, it wasn't too interesting, a sort of dictionary, but it was easy to stare at the pages and rest myself and keep my mind numb and let my eyes flutter and my head nod, everything getting soft around me and hazy and tired.

The librarian woke me up, shaking my shoulders. My eyes flew open and I was instantly awake because I always leap out of my sleep quickly.

She was a pretty thing, a young one, and she looked all nervous and worried as she bent over me. "Mister," she said, "you've got to wake up. It's closing time . . ."

My head ached and my eyes felt raw and strained as if I had let somebody borrow my own and had a pair that didn't fit. I'd been having a terrible dream that I couldn't remember. My mouth tasted acid and my teeth hurt although that was silly because how could false teeth hurt you? My gums, maybe.

The librarian looked frightened and I was sorry I had scared her. "What time is it?" I asked, to say something and put her at ease.

"It's five minutes to nine," she said, not standing too close to me. "If I hadn't come down here by chance, you'd have been locked in for the night . . ."

I leaned against the bookshelf to steady myself. "I'm sorry I gave you a scare," I said. "I belong to the bird watchers' society, you know, and I've been up since five o'clock this morning and must have got pretty tired." It scares me sometimes to think how I can lie so easy, like turning on a faucet. She still looked uncertain and I realized that we might be alone in the building and I figured the best way to make her feel better was to leave as soon as possible. That's a terrible thought: thinking that the best way to make somebody feel better is to leave them as soon as possible.

I tried to walk away from her with dignity, holding myself erect as I went up the stairs, but those damn bottles were jiggling and banging all over the place.

There's nothing better than an omelet and a glass of milk when your stomach is upset, at least that's what my mother always said. That's what I ordered at a place downtown, a sort of variety store-restaurant combination. Although I didn't have any appetite, my stomach was hollow and I knew that food was necessary to keep me going even if I didn't know where I was going: to the Rainbow Hotel, maybe. I sat at a table near the big plate-glass window and looked out at the street, at the people passing. Some of the store windows were lit up, and it's a lonesome thing seeing the store windows bright and the mannequins standing around all dressed up and knowing that there's nobody in the stores. I would have felt better if they shut off those lights at night: I never liked to see a light burning where there's nobody around. And the mannequins reminded me of Baptiste and his dolls.

I called the waitress over and ordered a strawberry shortcake, my favorite dessert, thinking that it might revitalize my appetite. She said there was no whipped cream left and didn't pay much attention to me. She was a young girl, no older than a high-school kid, and she was flirting and glancing at a young fellow wearing a T-shirt at another table. I ordered a piece of pie, anything at all, and she nodded and walked away.

I felt like talking to somebody. There was no book I could

bury my thoughts in and I didn't feel like taking out my little black book. The other people in the place were busy eating quickly, the way they do in night places like that. I wondered who I could talk to. There was poor Baptiste in his room on the other side of the square but I had told him I was leaving town and my appearance would upset him. Besides, those dolls would only get on my nerves. I wondered what Charlie and Gladys were doing; probably getting ready to go on their honeymoon, packing their clothes and giggling and maybe stealing a kiss although I hoped Gladys wouldn't get any lipstick on Charlie's collar because he'd get all upset.

I scolded myself for feeling bad: I had my health and plenty of money in my wallet and tomorrow was Memorial Day and the parade would go swinging by and on Friday I would get that job with the highway department and find a nice place to live and settle down. My own boss and nobody to tell me what to do.

The thoughts lifted my spirit but I still felt like talking to someone, someone who *knew* me, that I wouldn't have to introduce myself to. I was wishing that somebody would go by on the sidewalk and look in and recognize me and wave.

I thought of Emily Breault and how she'd waved at me that morning from the bus, and at the same moment I saw the telephone booth in the corner. Why not call Emily up? I thought. I found some coins in my pocket and went to the booth.

The buzzer sounded at the other end and I closed my eyes, hoping that she was home. After a long wait I heard her voice: "Hello, hello . . ."

That was Emily, all right. When I heard her repeat the greeting I remembered her old habit of saying almost everything twice. She used to be a teacher in a grammar school and she always acted as if you really didn't understand her unless she said a thing two or three times.

"How are you, Emily? It's me, Tommy Bartin," I said, feeling warm and happy to be talking to her and hearing the sounds of the tenement: water running and a voice calling someone and music from that little pink radio she kept near the kitchen sink.

"Well, Tommy Bartin," she said and you could hear how pleased she was. "I saw you today. Did you see me? I waved to you from the bus. Did you see me wave?"

"You bet I did. And I was hoping you'd get right off that old bus and let me buy you an ice-cream soda . . ."

She giggled and I asked her about the family. She said everything was fine, everything was fine, and Harry was foreman of the shipping room at the shop, and Elizabeth, the oldest, was in the seventh grade and turning out to be very artistic, very artistic, and one of her paintings, a painting of a cat with kittens won a prize at the children's exhibit at the museum, and Carol was fine, too, although she'd had pleurisy something terrible during the winter, and she herself was fine, fine but had been putting on too much weight, eating like a pig all the time, and Harry had gotten over his hypochondriac stuff and had settled down and gotten an ulcer and had to drink gallons of milk, gallons, and he'd always hated milk.

It was nice hearing all the news although I felt bad for little Carol. Harry and Emily always favored Elizabeth because she was the bright one, talented and pretty, and little Carol was a thin, worried-looking child.

"Do you want to talk to Harry a minute?" she asked. "He's right here . . ."

Her voice was muffled as she called to Harry and I

thought how wonderful it was to know people like them and call them up.

"Well, I guess he's busy right now," she said, on the telephone again. "But he said to give you his regards, his best regards."

Harry was a fellow who never liked to talk on the telephone and I remembered how Emily always got on his nerves when she got involved in those long, gossipy calls in the evening.

"Well, I'm glad that everything is fine with you people," I said. "I hope Carol doesn't catch any more colds and get that pleurisy back . . ."

"Oh, she's good and healthy now, good and healthy," Emily said. I wondered if she was telling the truth because her voice had gone flat and maybe she didn't want to worry me, knowing how much I liked that little Carol.

I hadn't talked for so long that way on a telephone that I didn't know what to say for a moment or two.

"That was too bad about Miss Bein dying," I said. "She was a nice old lady."

"Yes, that was too bad about her. I always liked her even though she was a busybody. The landlord we've got now is a nice fellow—he's certainly spruced up the place. . . ." There was a silence and I heard a voice, Harry's voice it sounded like, in the background. "Just a minute, Tommy," she said, and her voice was muffled again.

I wondered why she hadn't asked me how I was and what I was doing and all the rest of it. People are funny that way today. I guess the world is moving too fast and they haven't got time for things like that. Even poor Baptiste hadn't asked me anything, either.

She was back on the line. "Well," she said, sounding

breathless. There was a pause while she caught her breath and I waited.

"Gee, it sounds good to hear your voice," I said. "You sound real good. How's everything at 'The Beehive'? Still a lot of things going on? Remember the times those people from Linsdale moved in, all those kids they had, and they didn't tell Miss Bein about them and sneaked them all in after dark, smuggled them up the stairs and everything?"

She didn't answer me for a moment because I guess she couldn't remember right away. "That's right," she said, after a while. "That was funny, all right . . ."

I tried to think of something else to say. "I'm fine," I said. "Everything is fine with me."

"Well, that's good, Tommy," she answered but it sounded like she was thinking of something else.

"Say, did I call at the wrong time?" I asked, feeling embarrassed. "Have you got company or anything?" She was too polite to tell me something like that when I hadn't talked to her for such a long time.

"Well, no, no," she said, drawing the words out. "It's just that . . . well, we *are* a little rushed because Harry and I are going out tonight . . ."

You've got to admire this new generation: they don't mind going out even if it's half-past nine at night.

"Say, Emily," I said, "do you need a baby-sitter? Remember how I used to baby-sit with the kids while you and Harry stepped out? I wouldn't mind at all . . ."

"Well," she said, acting surprised that I'd be willing to baby-sit. She and Harry always said I was the best sitter they could find, and they always wanted to pay me but I never took a cent, of course. "Tell you the truth, Tommy, a little girl that lives down the street is coming here. She always baby-sits for us . . ."

"It seems late for a little girl to be out," I said. "I wouldn't mind baby-sitting at all. I mean, it would be kind of nice to see the kids again. Are they still up?"

"Oh, no, they're in bed, Tommy, and you wouldn't be able to talk to them." She didn't say anything for a moment and I was happy with the hope that maybe she was thinking over my offer. Maybe she was thinking that it *was* kind of late to be going out and it would be better to have an older person with the kids.

"Wait a minute, Tommy," she said. "I think there's somebody at the door . . ."

That's Harry for you. He'd never get up to open the door but would make Emily leave an interesting telephone conversation to see for herself. I heard her voice again, indistinct and blurry, and I guess she was arguing with Harry, telling him to answer the door himself.

She was back again. "Oh, Tommy, it's the insurance man," she said, crestfallen. "We've been meaning to take out more insurance and told him to stop in some night . . ."

Isn't that just like an insurance man, stopping in at that hour without any warning and on the night before a holiday?

"Well, I hope he doesn't hold you up from going out," I said. "You young people need to get away from the house and kids once in a while . . ."

"Well . . . he's just dropping off some material for us to look at. We'll be able to go out just the same," she said.

"I guess you're really all fixed up with a baby-sitter then," I said, trying to bring the subject around to my offer in a sly way.

"Well, Tommy, this girl is planning on it. What I mean is

. . . she needed some money the other day, some money to buy something or other and we advanced her the money, Harry is good that way, and now she feels she owes it to us. I mean, she feels she owes us a debt . . ."

That surprised me because Harry was never a generous person, too worried about himself all the time. Emily was talking hurriedly now about how important insurance was and I couldn't blame her for being in a rush, with the insurance man at the door and everything and Harry so helpless.

"It was nice talking to you, Tommy," she said, "really nice talking to you . . ."

"Same here," I said. The telephone is a wonderful instrument when you stop to think about it.

"Well, all right then, take care of yourself," she said.

"You know me, Emily. I'm always fine. Everything is fine with me. What the hake. I had a gallstone attack a while back but outside of that I hardly ever been sick a day in my life . . ."

"Yes, well, all right, you take it easy now," she said.

"You, too," I replied. You could see that she hated to hang up. "Say hello to Harry and the kids and I hope little Carol gets along good. Tell her to stay out of drafts. Now you hang up, don't keep that insurance man waiting for the sake of somebody like me. We can talk any time . . ."

"All right," she said. "Good-bye, Tommy." She sounded sad about something when she hung up, as if she wished we could have gone on talking awhile. I replaced the receiver, thinking how even at this moment Emily was probably feeling bad because she'd forgotten to tell me to call again and things like that always bothered her because she was always nice to everyone and hated to hurt anybody's feelings.

I stared at the telephone: why, I could call California if I felt like it, if I knew anybody in California. I thought of Baptiste and how much better off he would be if he had a telephone in his room and could call up somebody.

And I got all excited suddenly about an idea: why not call up Mr. Jones and tell him about Baptiste and ask him if he could go live at the infirmary? At the infirmary, he would probably forget all about his dolls because his trouble was being lonesome, that was all, and there would be other people there his age. I got more excited by the minute and fumbled the dime as I slipped it into the slot. The telephone buzzed and I waited, hoping Mr. Jones would answer, and that he wouldn't be too angry about Annabel Lee going away with the motorcycle boys and the way I'd left The Place without signing out, and not coming back.

"Hello, hello." It was Mr. Jones at the other end of the line and hearing his voice suddenly jolted me. Suppose he couldn't help Baptiste and suppose he took one step into Baptiste's room and saw those dolls and had him carted away to an asylum? I mean, Mr. Jones was still a young man in a way, only fifty or so, and he probably wouldn't understand that the loneliness had driven Baptiste to his crazy life with the dolls.

"Hello . . . anybody there?" Mr. Jones asked.

"It's me, Tommy Bartin," I said. I knew that I couldn't tell him about Baptiste: it would be taking a chance on betraying my old friend.

"Tommy, where are you? Are you all right? Why haven't you come back?" he asked and I could picture him sweating all over the place and to tell the truth my own hands were sweating, the telephone receiver wet in my grip.

"Oh, I'm all right, Mr. Jones," I said. "I'm fine. I guess you know I decided to leave The Place after all . . ."

"Well, Tommy, we can't keep anybody here against their will, you know. I only hope you're not doing anything foolish . . . I mean, you're not a young man anymore."

Why are people always talking about age? A man is as young as he feels. But I didn't want to be fresh with him or sassy.

"Oh, everything is great, Mr. Jones," I said. I didn't really feel like talking to him because he sounded sad and his voice brought back all the sadness of The Place and I could almost smell that strange odor that clings to the walls and the ceilings and the furniture there. "I got a job all lined up and a nice place to live and everything and plenty of money . . ."

"Yes, Stretch told me about the money, how Sweet Mary gave it to you. You deserved it, Tommy. You always treated her good. We're going to miss you, Tommy. You always were well thought of here . . ."

There was a pause and I heard him sigh, softly, and I could tell there was something wrong.

"Mr. Jones, is everything all right? You sound . . . kind of funny. Is Annabel Lee all right? Has anything bad happened?" I figured something bad must have happened because I had been sure he would ask me to go back and he didn't sound interested at all.

He didn't answer for a moment and I looked out through the window of the booth at the quiet, empty street. Even though I wouldn't have returned, I was wishing he'd have asked me to go back.

He still wasn't answering. "Say, Mr. Jones, Annabel Lee is all right, isn't she? I mean, nothing happened to her or anything?"

"No, no, she didn't have an accident or anything like that,

Tommy. We got her back safe and sound . . . safe, anyway. It's hard to explain, really . . ."

Small, cold snakes crawled under my skin. I heard the sound of motorcycles bruising the night outside the restaurant but I wasn't sure whether the motors were racing only in my mind. Don't let there be anything wrong with her, I prayed, don't let there be anything wrong.

"What do you mean, Mr. Jones?"

"Well, she's innocent, you know. You know how innocent she is . . . just a child, really. I mean, we always protected her from knowing what the world was really like. She's a baby in many ways, still believes in Santa Clause . . ."

Please God, I prayed, don't let it be anything bad that happened to her. Please.

"She went along with them on the ride and I guess it was great fun for her. That fool leader, Rudy Ludger I guess his name is, he's one of those crazy daredevils and he took her over some wild bumps but she got a kind of kick out of *that*. She always loved the roller coaster and has never had any sense of danger . . ."

The sound of motorcycles kept approaching, getting closer, just as his voice kept getting closer to the truth that I didn't want to hear. I looked out of the booth as two motorcycles sputtered past the restaurant. I wanted to rush out of there and follow them but I had to listen to Mr. Jones tell me about Annabel Lee.

"Anyway, I guess this Rudy fellow stopped for a while away from the others and got her by herself somewhere. That much I got out of her. I don't know what he did . . . in fact, I guess he really didn't do much at all, maybe kissed her a bit or touched her a little. It's hard to tell because she won't say a word about it. But the upshot was that the police felt I ought to have her examined by a doctor, to make sure she was all right, that nothing had happened. You know what I mean, Tommy?"

"Yes, I know what you mean, Mr. Jones," I said, thinking of that poor child.

"Anyway, the doctor examined her and she's all right, nothing happened, but ever since the doctor left, she's been crying up in the apartment and nobody's been able to do anything with her. Inconsolable. The doctor gave her a sedative but she hasn't fallen asleep and he said that she's just had some kind of shock, something that sort of jolted her out of her dream world a little bit, maybe a flash of what the world is really like or what things would be like if she was normal. In other words, she's had a taste for the first time of . . . I don't know . . . maybe terror or panic . . ."

I thought of her crying, nobody able to comfort her. I had never seen her really cry, only a few tears staining her eyes when she scratched herself or bumped her head or something like that.

"I'm sorry, Mr. Jones," I said. "I should have warned you a long time ago about those motorcycle fellows and how she was aching to go for a ride with them."

"Don't blame yourself, Tommy. The doctor said that something like this was bound to happen sooner or later, some little flash of insight that would affect her. Only, I hate to see her crying and not being able to do anything about it." He was quiet for a moment, and when he spoke again his voice was hoarse. "She doesn't seem to want any men around her and she clings to Minnie all the time and looks at me as if I were a stranger . . ."

"How about that Rudy What's-His-Name?" I asked. "The

police do anything to him? Are they going to make him pay for this, take him into court and fix it so he can't do anything like this again, maybe take his motorcycle from him?"

"There's nothing the police can do, Tommy," Mr. Jones said. "The examination showed that she . . . she hadn't been touched in a way that would make it a crime. And all the motorcycle boys said that *she* was the one who wanted to go for a ride, nobody forced her. It's really her word against his. And the word of a girl like Annie wouldn't stand up. And I wouldn't put her through the ordeal of court or anything . . ."

"You don't know how bad I feel about this, Mr. Jones. I'd give a million dollars if it hadn't happened . . ."

"Well, Tommy, something was bound to happen sooner or later. I mean, she's been going along thinking that the world was a wonderful place and that everyone was nice and Santa Claus came every Christmas and the Easter Rabbit on Easter morning and little by little she's got to find out about life . . . but it's too bad it had to happen this way . . ." I heard a voice in the background and then he said: "Minnie's calling me, Tommy. Annie's starting to quiet down and I guess I better go up to her . . ."

"You go right up to her," I said.

"Tommy . . . you sure you're doing the right thing? You sure you won't come back?"

"I've got to make my own way, Mr. Jones. I mean, a man has to find his own way, know what I mean?" I was wishing that I could put it all into words for him but the words still wouldn't come.

"Well, any time you change your mind you're welcome back, Tommy," he said. "Just ring the doorbell and we'll be glad to have you . . ."

"Good-bye, Mr. Jones," I said. "I hope Annie's all right. . . ." I was going to ask him to tell Annie that I was inquiring about her but I felt like an outsider suddenly, cut off from all of them, and Mr. Jones had said that she didn't want to have anything to do with men anymore. Please let her love her father again, I prayed, and kiss him good night.

"Good-bye, Tommy," he said and hung up.

I went back to my table and found that the waitress had put a ham sandwich at my place instead of the dessert I'd ordered. I wrapped it in a napkin and put it in my pocket along with the nip bottles I had forgotten to throw away and paid my check and stepped out the door.

And I stood there wondering where I could find those motorcycle fellows, especially the one they called Rudy.

Two motorcycles were parked in front of that place called the Harbor Arms: I could see them from across the street and I hurried in that direction, thinking of Annabel Lee crying up in her room and nobody able to console her. The streets were pretty deserted now, the shoppers all gone home except for a few stragglers. The Common across the wide street was dark and empty, the big veiled monument looking like a bandaged finger. The electric clock in the traffic circle said 9:58.

As I drew near to the motorcycles, I saw how lethal they looked, more like weapons of war than playthings that you take a young girl out riding on. Music blared out of the Harbor Arms and the neon sign blinked off and on, red and green, stop and go, red and green, making me pause a minute to catch my breath.

The placard with the pictures of the girl called Tootsie Rolle stood on the sidewalk. There were six or seven pictures of her, a blond girl in tights and a brassiere, standing this way and that. I remembered how we used to take the train to Boston in the old days and go to the Old Howard and watch the girls prancing around on the stage and how that pleasant glow always came over me, the hot throb that was part pain and part pleasure in my loins. I chuckled, thinking of the people at the infirmary, especially Harry Herman, who always liked the women, and how surprised they'd be to see me standing there looking at the pictures of a half-naked girl. That would show them how old I was: not old at all.

I looked at the motorcycles again and thought of Annabel Lee and I pushed my way through the door, hoping that Tommy the bartender wasn't still on duty. I mean, he had seen me fall on my face and I would just as soon avoid him.

He was at the bar, all right, looking bored and tired and so busy serving up the drinks that he didn't notice me. I stood inside the door for a minute, inspecting the place and the people, trying to spot the motorcycle fellows, looking for fellows with leather jackets or sideburns. There were a lot of people, fellows and girls and older men and women but nobody that looked as if they had just gotten off a motorcycle.

There was a jukebox playing but the music clashed with some other music coming from behind the double doors at the end of the bar where the nightclub was. And I figured that the motorcycle boys must be in there because they would be the type to go in and watch a half-naked woman dancing around.

Everything in the nightclub was blue: blue mirrors on the walls, the kind of mirrors they used to have in parlors in the old days, and a blue plush carpet that made you feel as if your feet were sinking into the floor, and blue upholstered chairs and a blue spotlight fastened on a fellow on the stage who was telling jokes.

A waiter in a blue vest approached me, an expression on his face that showed he expected me to tell him I was lost or else looking for the gents' room. I remembered the suave manners of actors in the movies who always slipped a bill to the headwaiter and I moved fast, reaching into my pocket but all I felt there was the ham sandwich from the restaurant. I didn't dare dig into my other pocket because I still hadn't thrown away those empty nip bottles. Anyway, he raised his eyebrows and I managed to say: "A table for one," remembering *that* from the movies, too, and he took me to a small table, about the size of a dime, next to the wall at the back of the place.

I didn't mind being so far back because it gave me a chance to look around for the motorcycle boys but the light was so dim that you could hardly recognize anybody. I squinted into the blue dimness but the people were only shadows and they all looked the same as they sat there, laughing and giggling.

What everyone was laughing at was the comedian on the stage, dressed in a striped suit and a straw hat and a bow tie that lit up at the end of a joke. I had to chuckle at that: there had been a fellow like him appearing with a medicine show in town probably thirty or forty years ago, dressed the same way. The jokes this fellow in the nightclub was telling weren't the same, however. They were all about cripples and children shooting their own parents and people with cancer and I couldn't see the humor in topics like that but everybody else did and laughed. I laughed because a man feels foolish sitting with other people like that without joining in whatever they're doing. Then he told a terrible joke, if you could call it a joke, about the Holy Virgin Mary, and I flinched as if someone had slapped my face. Laughter roared in the room and a young fellow at the next table jumped up and down in his chair, giggling. He caught my eye and I started laughing, too, as if the joke was really a joke and really funny, and even while I laughed I felt like I had plunged into a black sin but I kept laughing anyway until I began to cough, hating myself and everybody else.

The waiter stood by my table, waiting for me to order. I said, "A Tom Collins, my good fellow," the first thing that came to mind. The comedian kept up his chatter but I wasn't interested in him anymore, or in any jokes he had to tell. After a while, I realized that he wasn't very young and was probably fifty-five or sixty years of age. He wore heavy make-up that looked as though he spent all his time sunning himself and if you watched close and shut your ears to what he was saying, you could see that even *he* didn't think the jokes were funny because his eyes never looked merry. He kept wiping his forehead with a handkerchief, not wiping it exactly but dabbing away as if afraid that the make-up would come off and he would be revealed as a man of fifty-five or sixty telling terrible jokes in front of everybody.

My drink wasn't even half gone before the waiter came and stood beside my table again. He didn't look at me or at the stage or any place in particular but I could tell he was standing there waiting for me to order. I gulped down the drink and barely moved my head when he looked down at me, waiting for the order. I figured maybe he earned his money by commissions, so I ordered another Tom Collins although they're too sweet and womanish.

The comedian went into a song and dance and it was the saddest thing you could imagine. In the first place, the orchestra wasn't really an orchestra but three young fellows sitting on the stage behind him, and I didn't even notice them before, what with the lights dark and the blue spotlight on the comedian. They played the drums and guitar and piano and they were young enough to be grandsons of the comedian and when he started to dance and sing about "Bill Bailey, Won't You Please Come Home?" those young fellows kept glancing at each other in an amused way and it seemed like they were poking fun at him with the music. The comedian huffed and puffed and beads of perspiration stood out on his brow and his tan make-up started to leak and nobody in the audience paid him any attention but began to talk among themselves. I finished my drink and was glad to see him leave the stage. I felt so bad for him that I clapped loud and long when he left even though he'd told those terrible jokes, but the people who enjoyed his jokes so much didn't clap at all.

The lights turned on bright for a flashing moment. I looked around quick to see if I could spot the motorcycle fellows, but everybody looked the same in that swift instant before the lights were turned down again. A voice from backstage called: "Tootsie Rolle," in a mysterious way and there was a ruffle of drums. The voice continued: "And because this is the night before Memorial Day, Tootsie has a special holiday treat for you . . ."

I got a little angry about that because a nightclub is no place for that kind of stuff, Memorial Day being a serious holiday and not like the Fourth of July, and I almost rose to come out of the place in disgust but the waiter came and stood by my table again, his hands behind his back, waiting, and I wondered why he didn't go stand beside some other table for a while. Anyway, I ordered another Tom Collins.

The drums rolled again and the spotlight turned pink and Tootsie Rolle came dancing out. The music was soft and low, the drums beating gently, and Tootsie sort of glided in, dancing slowly and yet every part of her somehow moving. She was completely dressed up in a full pink gown with long sleeves and everything, but it fitted her tightly and she was a pretty husky girl. Her eyes were tired and red and she didn't look anything like the pictures out front or maybe she had looked like that a long time ago. She moved around on the stage awhile, not doing anything in particular, and I think she would rather have been back in her motel room, reading a book probably.

Then she seemed to come to life and her eyes brightened and got flirty and she started to fiddle around with the back of her dress and off it came, bingo, just like that, with no warning or hint of what was coming. She just stepped out of the dress and held it before her, stiff as a board. The old comedian puffed out and took it from her, and everybody whistled and applauded.

I'm no expert at the striptease or anything but it seemed kind of cheap somehow. I mean, the way she stepped out of her dress, automatic, without any warning or anything, as if she was bored and tired. Anyway, she stood there at the center of the stage looking at us. She had nothing on but her high-heel shoes and black net stockings and blue tights shining with sequins and a thin blue brassiere that barely held in her big bosom. She was a husky girl, all right, and a kind of sigh shivered through the room. The music got louder and the drums began to roll and Tootsie did something with her hand, reaching behind her, and all of a sudden two little American flags popped up, one on each side of her brassiere, as if she'd pressed a button. The music stopped and Tootsie called out in a squeaky, high-pitched voice: "Happy Memorial Day, everybody . . ." like it was New Year's Eve. All the people started clapping and whistling and laughing—that was the big Memorial Day surprise, I guess, although I imagine not too many people were looking at the flags. I mean, those flags sort of pulled down her brassiere.

It was kind of disgusting, to tell the truth, but I didn't

have time to think about it because the waiter came over and stood beside me and the music exploded again, the drums and saxophone joining in a frantic duet and Tootsie Rolle got serious and started dancing fast, her lips wet and parted and her breathing coming hard and she was rubbing her hands all over her body, her legs and thighs and stomach, and even the waiter seemed to forget about me and stood there watching her.

The music softened, like a whisper in the background, and Tootsie started to sway slowly, her stomach revolving in some clever way. She turned her back and began to do the same thing twitching around in rhythm, and the drums were beating loud but slow, as if the jungle surrounded us, and you could feel everybody in the place leaning forward, even the women, and then Tootsie began to shake all over, everything moving at once, and I thought how she would have made a fine acrobat if she'd put her mind to it.

And I thought: What's the matter with you, Tommy Bartin? Here's a big, husky woman, half-naked on the stage, and all you can do is think what a fine acrobat she'd make. You wouldn't have thought of that in the old days. You'd have been all hot and bothered by now. But I wasn't all hot and bothered, I was cool as a cucumber. I began to concentrate for all I was worth on her: her bulging legs and sweating thighs and the bursting brassiere. She whirled around again, bending over, and I could see a tear in her black net stockings and thought how terrible that was for her, standing in front of everybody with a rip in her stocking.

At that same moment, I happened to glance at a table across from me that was half hidden by some sort of rubber plant. The glint of hobnails, the kind the motorcycle boys wear on their jackets, caught my eye. I craned my neck and saw two fellows wearing those imitation officer hats—they didn't even take them off inside a nightclub, for crying out loud—and I forgot all about Tootsie Rolle and the music and pushed myself up from the table.

The lights and the drinks made me unsteady as I weaved my way across toward them. I bumped into a table that was so small that the fellow sitting there with a girl just picked it up and held it away while I went by.

"Where's your leader, that Rudy What's-His-Name?" I said, tapping one of the fellows on the shoulder. He was so engrossed with Tootsie up there on the stage dancing around that I had to hit his shoulder roughly and raise my voice. "Where's Rudy?" I asked again. "Where can I find him?"

The motorcycle fellow turned around and stared at me as if I was a crazy man or something. "Don't bother me, dad-dyo," he said. "I'm busy watching the lady . . ."

"Look, fella," I said, dizzy from the drinks in me, "I'm trying to find Rudy. Do you know where he is?"

"Do you think she'll take off that bra, pop?" he asked, his eyes glued on the stage. "This is her last night here and they say she's gonna take off that bra and let us see the promised land . . ."

I hooked my fingers in the collar of that black jacket and turned him to face me. "You can look at that bra all you want later but right now I want to know where Rudy is. Isn't Rudy the leader of all you fellows?"

The other motorcycle boy looked up at me now, and you could see he hated to take his eyes from the stage. "We had a tough day, daddyo," he said. "Riding all the way to Medford and back . . . let us enjoy the scene peaceful-like. Man, look at the scene yourself . . ."

"Who're you? Rudy's father or something?" the first fellow asked, half turning his face toward me but keeping his eyes on the stage, where Tootsie must have been doing something extra special because the music had gotten so soft you could hardly hear it and the air was heavy with a kind of nakedness to it, almost a shame in the atmosphere.

"Tell me where Rudy is and you can watch the bra come off," I whispered.

"Try the Silver Palace, man," the second fellow said. "He beat a retreat to the Palace a while ago . . ."

"Where's the Silver Palace?" I asked.

The first fellow turned to me with a pained expression on his face. "You want a road map, pop? Down on Water Street you'll find it. Man, everybody knows the Silver Palace. Hey, look at that . . ." he said. I thought: No wonder she has to go out and get drunk, with all these people in the audience acting like animals.

I stumbled through the club, brushing against tables again, but nobody seemed to notice because they were too busy watching Tootsie Rolle. The waiter was standing by the door, waiting for me with my bill in his hand, looking suspicious as if he thought I was trying to sneak out of there without paying. I barely glanced at the bill and handed him five dollars, waving the money at him like a big shot to show him that I wasn't just a derelict or something.

"Keep the change," I said, carefree suddenly. And I felt carefree because I had a destination now: I was going after those motorcycle fellows and make them pay for what they had done to Annabel Lee.

The air in the bar was heavy with the smell of beer and cigarette smoke but it seemed cool and refreshing after the blue atmosphere of the nightclub. I closed the door to the club and the music became fainter and the lights in the bar watered my eyes. The place was almost empty: most of the people were inside watching Tootsie Rolle, I guess. But there was some excitement near the door. It's funny how you can tell about excitement even when it's only some people standing around. Maybe it was the policeman standing there with the bartender and a couple of other fellows. When you see a policeman outside on the street, you don't think anything about it but a policeman *inside* a place has a different look to him.

I wanted to get to the door without Tommy seeing me and I started to slip past them, my face averted. Then I heard the cop say: "Well you never know, there's a lot of queer ones in the world. I picked up a guy last week and he was wearing a bra and panties, for crice sake." He was a young cop with a red face and freckles and he seemed out of place in a uniform. "But this one . . ."

I tried to brush past, and Tommy the bartender said to the policeman: "Yeah, but what about the dolls, Artie? What the hell was he doing with all those dolls?"

I stopped, frozen in my tracks.

"You got me," the policeman said. "If I could explain all the queer things in the world, I wouldn't be a cop on a beat . . ."

"What's this you're talking about?" I managed to gasp, my breathing heavy all of a sudden.

The sound of the drums was suddenly loud from the club and a fellow at the telephone in a booth near the door was arguing with somebody he kept calling "Baby."

The cop and the bartender and the others didn't look surprised when I spoke up. That's what I like about saloons: whether they're fancy or not, everybody accepts everybody else and you can have conversations, sometimes really nice ones, even with strangers.

The cop said: "This old guy in a room on the other side of the square. He killed himself tonight, slashed his wrists with a razor, and we found him in a room full of dolls . . ."

"He even had a doll sitting on the toilet, her pants down," one of the fellows said. "On the toilet, for the love of mike."

The room tilted as if the earth had come to a screeching halt and then started up again.

"Hey, you okay?" the cop said, his voice distant and hollow.

"You gonna take another dive, mister?" the bartender asked. "He took a real dive this afternoon, right on his face . . ." His voice sounded bubbly, as if he was talking underwater.

I groped for the door, my knees trembling, sickness twisting my stomach. The cool air outside burned my eyeballs and I steadied myself with one hand against the building. A fellow and a girl passing by looked at me curiously. I had a feeling the cop and the others were standing at the door watching me and I began to walk away, as fast as I could, my head as light as a balloon. I reached an alley and went inside and vomited, thinking: I must have heard wrong, that cop didn't get it straight, Baptiste would never do a thing like that, maybe it was some other man, maybe this thing about dolls is a new phase, something new going around like things that get popular once in a while, like that old game Knock, Knock, Who's There? and I knew those thoughts were crazy but I couldn't believe that Baptiste, the best damn rubber in the shop who could lick any three men with one hand tied behind his back, would do a thing like that. I'll see for myself, I said, hearing my voice and not caring if I was talking out loud, I'll go over there and he'll invite me in and we'll sit there talking and I won't mind the dolls at all as long as he's still alive and safe . . .

A police cruiser drove slowly away from the curb as I approached the doorway of Baptiste's apartment building. Two or three people were still hanging around, stragglers, the kind you always find remaining at the scene of a disaster or a tragedy long after everyone has gone. A woman stood on the steps of the doorway, her hair up in pin curls and a loose bathrobe dangling from her skinny body. She kept shaking her head and saying: "I can't believe it. Why, just this afternoon I said, 'Hello, how are you?' when he came up the stairs and he didn't answer as usual . . ."

Everybody avoided her eyes. A young fellow in a suede jacket nudged another fellow with his elbow, finding it all amusing, and a middle-aged couple acted embarrassed as if they wanted to leave but were being held there against their will. An old man stood slouched with his hands in his pockets, acting sad and disappointed that all the excitement was over.

"I won't get a wink of sleep tonight," the woman said, addressing the crowd, talking on as if she was being paid to keep them there, to hold their interest.

It was true then: poor Baptiste. I had an urge to yell out at the woman that Baptiste had been a sick man and lonesome, and if they'd all been nicer to him and treated him decent and kind maybe it might not have happened.

The door pushed open and the woman with the fat stomach and the nice voice stepped out, her face still greasy with cold cream. She put her arm around the other woman and said: "Come on up, Edna. It's all over . . . the policeman said for us to go inside and settle down or this'll go on all night . . ."

Edna sniffed and I turned away, the weakness overcoming me once more.

"You there," the woman with the cold cream called. "You're the one I was telling the police about. You was here this afternoon . . ."

I turned back in surprise but tried to remain in the shadows. Everyone was looking at me and you could feel the excitement rising.

"You was the one went to his room this afternoon and started him hollering and yelling," she cried, pointing at me with the longest finger I ever saw, her voice shrill as a whistle. She turned to her friend in the bathrobe. "He's the one, Edna. We left the poor man alone at least, but this one came here and got him all upset . . ."

"You made a mistake, lady," I said, backing away. But a mailbox at the edge of the curb halted my retreat.

"Don't give me that, mister," she said, her skin shining in the yellow light. "I saw you with my own two eyes. You went in that room and he started yelling and you ran out of there and almost knocked me off my feet . . ."

You could hear the crowd beginning to murmur among themselves, taking it all in, something they could tell their friends and neighbors about the next day.

"Not me, lady," I said, trapped, wondering how to get away. "I just happened to be strolling by just now. I don't know what you're talking about . . ."

"Find a policeman, Edna; find a policeman," the woman shouted in a frenzy, beating the air with her fists.

"Where am I going to find a policeman, for heaven's sake?" the other woman asked, frightened and puzzled. You

could see that she didn't want to have anything to do with
this situation, her nerves were already frayed.

That gave me a little hope and I thought I might be able
to brazen it out.

"Look, lady," I said, trying to sound calm and reasonable.
"I just come from baby-sitting with my grandchildren, two
little girls, and I been at their house, my daughter's house, all
day. I could get her and prove it to you. It must have been
somebody looked like me . . ."

"I'd recognize that foolish sports coat of yours anywhere,"
she said.

"What does it matter?" the other woman asked, trying to
calm her down. "The man is dead, nothing will bring him
back. It's been bad enough . . . let's go up . . ."

"This fellow here probably caused it all," the woman said,
her voice harsh, not pretty at all as it had been, "running past
me and almost knocking me down. He's lying . . . and if a
man lies, he's liable to do most anything . . ."

"Let sleeping dogs lie, Hazel," her friend said, opening the
door. "It's getting chilly out here . . . let's go in and I'll
make you a nice hot cup of tea . . ."

The angry woman sagged suddenly, the fight gone out of
her, tears springing to her eyes. "That old Frenchman was
really a nice man," she said, "really a nice man . . ." She
allowed her friend to turn her around and point her toward
the doorway. At the last moment, she swiveled back and said
in a deadly voice, sharp as an arrow aimed at my heart: "Bet
if you hadn't come by here this afternoon, he'd still be
alive . . ."

"Lady, lady," I shouted, in anguish. "I didn't know him. I
didn't even know him . . ."

I barely recognized my own voice.

The door closed behind the women and I turned to the crowd. "What are you looking at, anyway?" I yelled. They were staring at me in a terrible way, their faces stark and yellow in the light from the lamppost. "Get away from here, go away, all of you . . ."

I turned and ran, everything a blur in front of my eyes, and a sob tore out of me from the pain of running so fast at my age, my blood throbbing in my ears, and I wouldn't have been surprised to hear a cock crow behind me.

THERE'S A DARK and lonesome spot in every town where the bright, shining stores come to an end and the buildings rise out of the darkness, the pale street lights flickering in the tree branches like candles for the dead. And that was where I found myself, gasping for breath, across the street from the run-down barroom with peeling letters in the dirty window that spelled: "SILVER PALACE BAR." Five or six motorcycles were parked outside and they seemed to be moving even when standing still.

I waited for my heart to stop hammering and my breathing to quiet down but I was afraid to stand still, to remain there in the night, afraid of my thoughts, afraid of calling up the image of Baptiste, and I ached for a drink more than anything else in the world.

I stalked across the street on my aching legs, keeping my mind a blank, wanting only a good stiff shot and a glass or two of beer. That would make everything seem better and I would be able to think clear and decide what to do. The door stuck as I opened it and it was necessary to fumble with the handle and I hate to enter a place that way, struggling with the door.

The bar resembled one of those old poolrooms that had been converted into a saloon, feeble light coming from old-fashioned green-shaded bulbs dangling from the ceiling as if the bulbs were being strangled by the cord and could only give off dying light. The booths were scarred and nicked, initials and swear words carved into the wood. The jukebox against the far wall at the back of the place was old and battered, no neon lights or anything.

The place was quiet but as I made my way to the bar, squinting in the pale light, I saw the motorcycle fellows clustered around a telephone. One fellow was talking into the telephone and you could hear his voice because there was no telephone booth.

The bartender was a fat, pale man with a worried face and he leaned on the bar, his chin resting on his hands watching the motorcycle fellows.

"A double shot and a beer chaser," I said, loud enough to rouse him, and he looked at me startled, as if I had awakened him from sleep.

"Hey, poppo, keep it quiet," one of the fellows near the telephone hissed at me, pointing to the boy who was doing the talking.

I wasn't in the mood to argue because the thought of Baptiste dead, bathed in his own blood, kept appearing in my mind, and I only wanted the drinks to chase away the picture. The bartender filled the glasses and took my money and whispered: "Don't argue with them. They're in an ugly mood tonight . . ."

I swallowed the whisky in two long burning gulps that smarted my eyes and seared my throat and then I flooded my mouth and throat with the beer. I sighed and hunched over the bar, waiting for the liquor to work.

The young fellows burst into laughter behind me, that tickled kind of laughter which showed that they had done something clever but I didn't pay much attention to them. Annabel Lee and what had happened to her had almost faded away, chased by the terrible vision of Baptiste, dead by his own hand.

I signaled to the bartender for another beer and he moved cautiously as if he didn't want to make a sound and placed the foaming glass on the bar. It was tap beer and ordinarily I don't trust the pipes in a run-down barroom, but I wasn't in a frame of mind to be fussy.

One of the motorcycle boys said: "Here, Teddy, get some change for the phone . . ."

"Okay, Rudy," a voice answered. I turned around, curious about that Rudy, and I saw him there, leaning against the wall near the telephone. I studied him and saw that he looked like an altar boy; he had a round, pink face with blue eyes, a scrubbed look about him, his features delicate except for thick lips that had a pout to them. It was hard to imagine him sitting on his motorcycle because he wasn't wearing his black jacket. His white shirt, a sporting type with blue around the collar, was neat and clean as if his mother had just pressed it. The other motorcycle fellows were young-looking, too, with eager faces. I thought: They don't look tough or wise or mean. Maybe they didn't do anything to Annabel Lee, after all. Maybe she's just a little hysterical from the experience and she'll be all right by tomorrow, everything forgotten like a bad dream.

Relief washed over me or maybe it was the drink working in me, because there's always a time when the liquor begins to take hold, humming in your blood and dancing in your head, and it gives a softness to everything, takes away all the sharp edges, and you feel as if you could make a wish with your eyes closed and the wish would come true.

The bartender had given the boy change for the telephone, and I ordered another shot, not wanting to lose the nice feeling. The bartender served me but kept his eyes on the boys, frowning, and he stayed nearby, polishing the top of the bar with the dirtiest rag I ever saw, shaking his head and muttering to himself.

I heard the coin tinkle into the telephone and a hush came over the place so that you could hear the swish of the rag, and I spread my elbows wide so that he wouldn't start wiping up the bar in front of me and probably sweep ten thousand germs there.

"Hello there, hello. I'm sorry to bother you at this late hour but there's something I thought you ought to know. . . ." I half turned and saw Rudy at the telephone, his voice soft and sincere. The other fellows were pressed close by him.

"No, lady, you wouldn't know me even if I gave you my name," Rudy said in a sweet, choirboy voice, "but you did me a favor a long time ago and I want to pay you back. You see . . . I saw—it hurts me to say this, madam, but you should know for your own good—I saw your husband not a half-hour ago in the lane out near the cemetery in the back seat of his car with a girl, a waitress at the Monument Restaurant, and they were both naked as the day they were born, going to town on each other. . . ." He paused, listening, his cherub eyes lifted toward the ceiling. "Yes, I know it's a terrible thing but I know you're a nice woman and I thought you should know. You should have seen them, naked, stark naked, and grunting and groaning . . ." He listened again and said: "Oh, I know it's hard to believe, lady, but believe me, I thought you ought to know. I just wanted to show you how much I appreciated that favor . . ."

He replaced the receiver on the telephone hook and his friends burst into laughter, slapping each other on the back and dancing around, and Rudy licked his thick lips and smiled in a lazy way at them.

The bartender threw his rag down on the bar and leaned across to me. "Those lousy kids, they ought to be arrested. Every night they're in here with their crazy antics . . ."

The motorcycle fellows wandered down to the end of the bar and put some money in the jukebox. Crazy, wild music filled the place.

"Well, at least they're trying to do right," I said, trying to keep my voice steady because the drinks were really working now and his face seemed to shimmer. "Even though it's none of their business. Now maybe that wife can talk some sense into that husband of hers and save their marriage . . ."

The bartender looked disgusted. "Don't you get it, old-timer? The husband's not out with another woman. They made it up. They check around at night and find out who's gone out, maybe a fellow bowling with his team from the shop or doing something else just as innocent. And then they call his wife and tell her those lies . . ."

"That's terrible," I said. "But why don't you tell them to stop it or throw them out or something?"

"Look, mister," he said. "I'm just trying to make ends meet in this rotten place. The kids would find out who blew the whistle on them—and then I'd be on the receiving end of worse than telephone calls . . ."

I thought: What a funny world, where grown men are afraid of a bunch of young punks.

"Give me another shot," I said. I thought of Annabel Lee at the mercy of those fellows and my head began to pound, not with pain but with anger. I looked down at them, where they were dancing together, horsing around in high spirits. Rudy was standing apart from them, his eyes bright and glittering, as if his mind was far away, remembering something. Remembering what? Remembering Annabel Lee and what he might have done to her?

I drank the shot but it couldn't blunt the anger.

"Pour me another," I said.

"You better take it easy, old-timer," the bartender said, raising his voice above the music and the noise the motorcycle fellows were making.

I slammed the glass down on the bar. "Don't call me old-timer," I said. "A man is as young as he feels . . . so I got a few gray hairs on my head, does that mean I have to be an old has-been? How old are you, fella, forty-five, fifty? But you let those wild kids walk all over you, coming in here every night, and you're too afraid to do anything about it."

I looked down at Rudy who was standing by himself, watching the others frolicking around, as if he was above all those foolish things and I thought of him touching Annabel Lee. The song in the jukebox ended at that moment and I yelled: "Hey, you, Rudy, Rudy What's-Your-Name, I've got a bone to pick with you . . ."

The dizziness returned as he looked at me in surprise and I had to clutch at the bar as I stepped off the stool. The music crashed through the air again but it died suddenly, cut off in a fading howl as one of the fellows yanked the plug off the wall. Rudy walked down toward me, slow and easy, a half-smile on his face, his blue eyes innocent and wondering.

"Did you call me, mister?" he asked, soft and sweet, as if I was the last person in the world that would call to him.

"That's correct, my boy," I said, getting control of myself and shaking my shoulders to stand erect.

"You better watch your step, pop," the bartender whispered, but I shrugged off his words, feeling strong and good and noble, everything under control. Maybe Baptiste was dead and maybe I had turned my back on him and denied him after he died but Annabel Lee was still alive and a lot of innocent girls, and poor women who would answer their telephones and hear a terrible, gentle voice whispering lies in their ears.

Rudy's friends followed him as he walked, slowly and lazily, toward me.

"What's the beef, poppo?" one of the other fellows asked, as he took a place beside Rudy. He was about seventeen years old, his face fresh with pimples but his eyes were old, without any age to them.

Rudy lifted his hand, silencing the boy. "I'm sorry, mister," he said to me. "I don't believe I know you . . ." He smiled at me, a question in his eyes and a light in them as well, as if he wished that he really knew my name so that we might be friends.

"It doesn't matter if you know me or not," I said. "But you know a girl by the name of Annie? A poor kid you took on a ride today to Medford?"

"He means the moron, the little cutie with the drip lip," the boy with the ageless eyes said.

Rudy turned to the boy in a sudden anger. "What's the matter with you, Leonard?" he asked, his voice hurt. "She wasn't a moron. She was a sweet little girl and she wanted a ride and we took her along for a ride . . ." He shook his head at the stupidity of that Leonard and looked at me again. "She's a sweet kid, mister," he said, sadly. "And when I realized she wasn't right, it really hurt, you know. And I thought: Why not give her a thrill, the thrill of a lifetime, bring a little bit of excitement to her life? Why, I treated her like she was my little sister . . ."

"Is that why she's up there at the infirmary crying her head off?" I asked. "She's hysterical up there and won't let anybody come near her . . ."

Rudy closed his eyes for a moment as if someone had slapped his face. He opened them and his big, thick lips pouted worse than ever. "Gollee, mister," he said, shaking his head, and he looked more like a choirboy than ever. "I'm sorry to hear that. She's such a sweet little thing. That's terrible. But she seemed to be having such a good time and it did my heart good to hear her laughing as we rode along on the open road . . ."

One of the fellows giggled and Rudy closed his eyes again, a vein throbbing in his temple, and he said: "Stop that, Roy. What's the matter with you? Don't you realize that we upset that poor little kid by taking her for a ride? And this fine man here is all upset about it too?"

The giggling stopped. Rudy looked at me again, a pained expression in his eyes. "I'm sorry, mister. Really. I don't blame you for being mad and everything. Believe me, when I realized that she was—what do they call it?—mentally retarded, I just about crumbled inside. All inside, you know? And I thought: Well, why not show her a good time? Why not take her to the meet and have her enjoy herself and probably buy her an ice-cream cone? No harm could come of that. And it would be something she would remember. The poor kid . . ."

You could see that he was a nice boy, really, and had probably gotten mixed up with all these wild fellows standing around him. But it was hard to think clear and I blinked my eyes, trying to bring everything into focus. He *seemed* like a nice boy, but how about those telephone calls the bartender said he made all the time? Yes, how about that telephone call he made a little while ago to that poor woman, telling all those terrible lies?

"I think you're fooling me," I said, studying him closely, half closing my eyes to make everything stand still.

"He thinks you're fooling him, Rudy," the boy called Roy said, a funny kind of anger in his voice, anger that was softened with a half-laugh. "Rudy don't kid nobody, mister. You don't kid nobody, do you, Rudy?"

"Why, I wouldn't think of fooling you, mister," Rudy said, looking injured. "Besides, you look too sharp, too shrewd to fool. A while ago I was looking at you sitting there at the bar and I said to Roy . . ." He turned for an instant toward the boy beside him . . . "Didn't I, Roy?" And he looked at me again. "I said, 'Doesn't that look like a smart fellow there at the bar, that nice gentleman sitting there?' "

A hiccup rolled out of my throat and I coughed. "Pardon me," I said. He was the first person who hadn't called me an old man for a long time and he was really a sincere-looking fellow.

"Why did you get mixed up with these terrible fellows?" I asked him softly, showing that the conversation was strictly between the two of us. "Why did you want to make that awful telephone call, telling lies to that woman? Did these fellows put you up to it?"

He looked around suspiciously, then winked at me and edged closer, lowering his voice to a whisper. "Listen, mister," he said, "I'll admit we fool around sometimes, calling people up. Just for a lark and we don't really do anything *mean* or low-down. But this call I made to that woman tonight, that was on the level. Honest. We really did see her husband out with that waitress in a car . . ."

His face had pleading in it, as if the most important thing in the world was my understanding, my belief in him. "I don't know," I said, unsure of everything, thinking of Baptiste and my own sins, the bad things I myself had done. Who was I to be a judge of anyone else?

"Do I look like that type of fellow?" Rudy asked. "Fool around, sure, but not hurt anybody. Once in a while, the fellows here in the bike club get a little restless and we have some fun, harmless fun, but never anything that would upset anybody. That's why I felt so bad when I saw you all upset about that nice little kid. Do you think if I bought her a present, something nice, maybe a doll or something, that would make her feel better?"

I touched him on the shoulder because he seemed so sad and regretful. "You tell him, Rudy," one of the fellows said, smirking. It just proves how bad companions can affect a boy, I thought.

"Look, mister, why don't you join us for a drink? Let me buy you a drink to show that there's no hard feelings?" Rudy asked, and the other boys joined in a chorus of voices, friendly suddenly, asking me to sit with them.

I hiccuped again, cursing silently, because it's hard for a man to act dignified when a hiccup pops out of his mouth.

"Listen, old-timer," the bartender called suddenly, "why don't you just come over here and have a nice quiet drink at the bar and keep me company? I'll give you one on the house . . ." He still had that worried look on his face and it always makes me feel bad to see a fellow who can't relax and enjoy himself.

Rudy turned to the bartender and spoke harshly. "Why

don't you mind your own business, buddy?" he said. "All we want to do is buy this nice fellow a drink. Is that against the law?"

The bartender's pale face flushed and he picked up that old rag and busied himself wiping the bar again. It felt nice to be popular like that, people wanting you to have a drink with them. I figured the poor bartender was lonesome, working in that run-down place with nobody intelligent to talk with, but I wanted to sit down with Rudy and his friends because I had a feeling I could make Rudy see the error of his ways, how he should turn his back on these wild, wise fellows and try to straighten out.

"What do you say, mister? Will you let me buy you a drink to make up for everything?" he asked.

My legs were still unsteady and I wasn't in a mood to drink any more, really, because the night was wearing on and I was afraid to check the hour. I still hadn't made any arrangements for sleeping that night and my mind was getting confused and weary, the thoughts of Annabel Lee and Baptiste chasing around in my brain. Yet I figured another drink might help me settle down and clear my mind, so I joined Rudy and his friends in a booth in the back of the place.

The boys were all friendly suddenly, in high spirits, and they were very polite, insisting that I enter the booth first. They jostled around, full of pep and energy, and they kept pushing each other so that I bruised my shoulder against the rough plaster wall a couple of times but I didn't want to say anything to spoil their fun. The booth was so crowded that Rudy pulled a chair over and sat at the end like a chairman presiding over a meeting, and he kept looking at me, smiling and happy, although I wished that he would calm the other fellows down so that we could talk quietly.

"Now, how about that drink?" Rudy called to me over the noise.

I was still a little tipsy from the shots and the beer but I shrugged. "All right," I said.

"And then we'll make another phone call," the one called Leonard said, or maybe it was the other one, Roy, because it was hard to tell them apart, to be honest. Except for Rudy, they all were still wearing their black jackets.

Rudy left to buy the drink for me and the words about the telephone call finally penetrated to my brain, which goes to show how liquor can dull your mind. "What do you mean, another phone call?" I asked them. "You boys should be ashamed of yourselves, doing things like that . . ."

"Aw, mister, don't be a square," one of the fellows said. "We just like to have a little fun. It's a holiday tomorrow, Memorial Day, and we just want to celebrate a little . . ."

I could hear Rudy and the bartender arguing about something or other. It was getting so late that I guessed the bartender probably wanted to close the place and go home.

"What's the use of a holiday if you can't celebrate?" another fellow said.

"Memorial Day isn't a holiday you celebrate with crazy antics," I said, thinking of Tootsie Rolle and those little flags on her brassiere. "It's a solemn occasion . . ." I looked at their young faces. None of them was more than twenty-one or twenty-two and a couple appeared young enough to be in bed sleeping at this hour. "And what have you fellows got to celebrate about, anyway? You were never in any war. Tomorrow they're honoring dead men, heroes, men who died to keep the world free. Tomorrow, they're going to unveil that monument there in the square and you fellows can look up and see a real man, a hero . . ."

"Hey, poppo, you're really hipped on this Memorial Day gig, huh?" the one called Roy said.

"It's a solemn day," I answered, wishing that Rudy would stop his arguing with the bartender so that he could help me make these fellows understand a little about how serious Memorial Day is.

"What good's a statue in the park?" one of the fellows asked. "All that money going for pigeon bait. Why, they could've built a big recreation center for us . . ."

"That's right," another fellow said. "A nice big recreation center so that us poor kids wouldn't have to be out on the streets, getting into all kinds of trouble . . ."

But it was hard to tell whether they were being serious or not because they kept winking at each other as they talked and nudging each other with their elbows and it was kind of sad, in a way.

It was sad because they were so young and I had a feeling that any one of them alone would be a nice boy but all together like that they had to *act* wise and everything.

"Well, a recreation center certainly would be a nice thing," I said, "and maybe someday they'll put one up. But right now there's a nice statue there and you fellows should show the proper respect . . ."

Rudy returned at that moment carrying my drink on a tray, and I had to admit that he certainly knew how to act, young as he was. The drink was in a fancy glass and he held it up in the air after he set down the tray. "Here, my good friend," he said, "is an extra special drink for a man who really has a heart. I mean, a man who worries about things, and there aren't enough people in the world like that today. I mean, a man who worries about us young fellows going

wrong and worries about little girls and women getting telephone calls . . ."

He leaned over and gently placed the glass in front of me,
careful not to spill anything. I had never drunk from such a
fancy long-stemmed glass before. "It looks like champagne,"
I said, and they all laughed, watching me closely, and you
could see how happy they were to be buying me a drink and
I thought again what a nice bunch of fellows they were when
you got to know them, despite all their bravado and wise
talk.

"And he worries about Memorial Day, too," Leonard said,
taking out a handkerchief and dabbing at a pimple that was
starting to bleed. You had to feel sorry for the poor boy with
those terrible pimples.

"He does?" Rudy asked, settling himself in the chair.

"Why, sure," Leonard said. "I'm afraid, Rudy old boy,
that we got him all upset because we want to celebrate the
holiday. He thinks only heroes got a right to celebrate . . ."

I put down the glass, figuring that I might as well set them
straight. "That's not what I said," I told them. "I said Memorial Day is a day for heroes, a day to honor the dead heroes
who gave their lives to make the world safe for democ-
racy . . ."

"Gee, that sounds interesting, mister," Rudy said. "Tell us
all about it. But first, have that drink and relax yourself.
Come on now, fellows, let's be quiet for a minute and let
him have that drink and then we'll find out about Memorial
Day . . ."

The other fellows quieted down and they all watched me
and you had to admit that Rudy was the leader, all right,
with qualities of leadership, as they say, because they always
did what he said.

I raised the glass to my lips and sipped slowly, hoping that it was champagne after all because I had never had any champagne. The liquor was sweet and sour at the same time and it tasted terrible, to tell the truth, but I didn't want to hurt their feelings. It wasn't a drink that would quench a man's thirst because it left a dryness in my mouth and throat afterward although it went down smoothly enough.

A kind of hushed silence fell on the booth as the fellows watched me put down the glass and I guess they were waiting for my speech about Memorial Day. I felt warm and secure suddenly, happy that I had met these fellows, because I hadn't given a thought to Baptiste or Annabel Lee for half an hour or so and I hadn't even been worried about finding a place to sleep. Maybe Rudy could help me get a room for the night.

"Go ahead, mister," Rudy said. "Tell us all about the holiday . . ." He was smiling at me gently, that innocent light dancing in his eyes, and the other boys were tense and quiet watching me and I felt as if I was on a stage, and it's a nice feeling with everybody watching you, waiting for you to speak.

I was afraid that a hiccup would spoil the moment but nothing happened. "All right," I said. And I began to tell them all about Memorial Day and how thousands of men had given their lives so that these young fellows could have nice homes and opportunities and be able to ride their motorcycles along the highways and how freedom had to be fought for. I heard my own voice echoing in my ears and it sounded strong and vibrant and I shut my eyes to listen to my words, and my tongue was thick with the words and the darkness swam around me and an edge of panic touched me and I opened my eyes and for some reason I felt that it was important to keep talking and Rudy's face, grinning and grinning, swayed in front of me and I wished I knew the Gettysburg Address and my eyes felt funny and my left hand was tingling and numb and Rudy's lips were wet, thick and wet, and I could hear my voice rising, trying to explain what that statue meant in the Common and how important it was, and I was suddenly lost, lost and alone, and I gripped the edge of the table to steady myself, to keep from falling into the darkness and I tried with all my strength to keep my eyes open so that darkness wouldn't overtake me but terrible bright lights exploded in front of me or maybe inside of me, behind my eyeballs, and a long scream gathered itself far away and I didn't close my eyes, I fought to keep my eyes open but the darkness began to close around me and I screamed at the end of a long tunnel, dark and hot, and nobody could hear and nobody could help me. . . .

EVERYTHING WAS GRAY when my eyes fluttered open. Heat and cold pressed against me, my forehead throbbing with a hot ache and the back of my head cold and numb. Purgatory must be like this, I thought, hot and cold and gray.

I lifted my head gingerly to see if the rest of my body was there. I seemed to be in some kind of coffin, although the sides weren't high enough for a coffin and there was no lid. I felt the side of the box with my hand, and cold stone chilled my fingers. A foul taste filled my mouth and a sour belch rolled up out of my stomach. I knew then that I was alive and still in the world because I figured people didn't burp in purgatory.

A voice suddenly shouted at me, loud and strong and angry, although I couldn't understand the words. I began to sweat with fear, the perspiration rolling down under my armpits. The fear pushed me to a sitting position and my head reeled as I moved. My head felt as if it had been taken off during the night and screwed back on again, some demon giving it an extra twist or two.

I dimly remembered running through the streets the night before after finding out that Baptiste was dead and that terrible bar with the shots of whisky and the motorcycle fellows at the telephone.

My hand groped in the grayness, touching something coarse and stiff: burlap, canvas? With my other hand I explored behind me and I touched coldness, a hard coldness, and I almost jumped out of my pants with fright: the thing I touched felt like a shoe, for crying out loud, a hard stone shoe.

That voice kept booming, the words echoing in the air, near and yet far away, all around me and yet nowhere, and the sweat on my brow turned cold, and I began to shiver.

I got accustomed to the grayness after a while and was able to focus, although my eyes burned with fire and my head throbbed. I was still dressed up in my Sunday trousers and my nice green-plaid sports jacket, and I jiggled my hands around, checking my pockets. My pockets were all empty and everything was gone: my wallet and my little black book and the little nip bottles and my best handkerchief. My money was gone with the wallet, the stake Sweet Mary had given me to start fresh again. I pounded my fist against my leg. Then I got a terrible feeling of being lost because the little card was gone along with my wallet, the card that said: "I am a Catholic. In case of an accident please call a priest . . ."

I thought: Get a good grip on yourself. I touched the canvas again and it was canvas, all right. I felt the other side of me and touched the cement and it was cement, all right. And that was certainly a shoe. I could feel the cement shoestrings and knew what they were although I had never touched cement shoestrings before. I don't think many people have.

I drew up my knees and put my arms around them to stop the trembling. The voice kept going on and I concentrated hard, trying to make sense out of the words but I was unable to recognize them. Suddenly a whine filled the air, a high screeching noise that reminded me of something. I pleaded with myself to remember what the whine was because it sounded familiar and reassuring. The whine . . . of course: the screech of a microphone or a loudspeaker when something goes wrong with the wires or controls, like at the meeting of the Happy Timers Club. But it was all crazy. I wondered who could be shouting at me through a microphone while I sat in a cement box with a piece of canvas hiding me.

A sensation of danger, the danger of falling, made me hug myself closer. Then I noticed a pinpoint of light in the canvas above my head, like a star in the grayness. I raised up to a kneeling position, fighting the strange sensation of space all around me. I stretched my neck and placed my eye against the small hole in the canvas where the light was coming in. Sunlight dazzled my eye and it blinked furiously for a few moments, obscuring my sight. Suddenly I could see clearly and I almost fainted dead away on the spot.

"For crying out loud," I whispered, and took my eye away, pushing my face against the canvas. Then I pressed my eye close to the hole again, and whistled.

There was the entire square below, crowded with hundreds of people: the band standing at attention in blue-and-white uniforms, the soldiers noble and erect with their rifles beside them, the little kids holding their parents' hands, old people and young people, and a boy who had shinnied up a telephone pole—all of them staring me right in the eye.

I drew away, dizzy, and knelt there for a moment listening to my breathing and the voice in the air. I looked again.

The crowd was still there. I raised my head a bit and looked sharply downward and saw the platform directly below me. A young fellow stood at the microphone talking, while some men, most of them bald-headed or with thinning hair (funny how seldom you see the tops of people's heads) sat behind him on those funeral-parlor kind of chairs. The boy's words made sense, at last. ". . . the people . . . shall not perish from the earth." He was the bright honor-roll student they always picked to recite the Gettysburg Address.

As he finished, the crowd applauded, the clapping thin and scattering in the open air. I watched the boy take his seat beside old Henry Pike, the oldest man in town, born on the day Lincoln was shot.

What am I doing here? I asked myself, realizing at last that I was crouched at the foot of the statue that was to be unveiled that morning. The cold hard stone was the foot of the statue, and I was trapped, ten or twelve feet above the ground, held in there by the canvas. The canvas was tight at my feet where a rope on the outside was probably tied to keep the canvas secure. How did I get here? I wondered. Did I climb up when I was wild with the drink? I've gotten into a few fights in my time when the drink was roaring in me and once I swam clear across Moosock Brook at its widest point and almost caught pneumonia, but I never was the kind of man who went climbing up statues.

I looked around at the crowd again . . . and I saw the motorcycle boys standing in front of the platform, and they weren't looking at the speakers or the officials. Their heads were tilted upward toward the statue itself, foolish grins on their faces. My vision blurred and I blinked hard and recognized Rudy standing in the midst of them, that dreamy smile on his face as he held his head erect. Those terrible fellows and their cruel jokes: they must have carried me here last night after I passed out from the drinking and somehow lifted me up the ladder. I thought of that strange, dry-tasting drink and suddenly knew that they must have put something in it to knock me out.

I looked around wildly, wondering how I could slip out of there without being seen. I felt the base of the statue where the canvas was tight and I couldn't tug it free. I crawled to the right and left a few feet but the box I was in ended at the edge of the front section. There was no ledge or any other kind of support at the sides of the base to creep around on.

I returned to the peephole and saw a big fellow with a bald head stride to the microphone. He held up his hands, and his voice boomed in the air, echoing to all corners of the square.

"Ladies and gentlemen," he called. "Honorable Senator and Mr. Mayor, Town Officials and Members of the Clergy, Soldiers and Sailors and Marines and Veterans of All Wars . . ."

His voice went on and on, and I turned my attention to the crowd, the faces all mixed together, and I shuddered. Everyone I knew in the world was probably out there, Stretch and Mr. Jones and Annabel Lee and all the people at The Place; and Harry and Emily Breault and their two children who always thought I was a special kind of fellow with poems at the tip of my tongue; and all the Happy Timers, Charlie and Gladys with them; and those old ladies at the rooming house were Baptiste had lived; and maybe poor Tootsie Rolle . . . and panic swept me again and I clawed at the canvas.

I began to cry, tears rolling down my cheeks, and I thought: I should have stayed at The Place because I hadn't done myself or other people any good by leaving. Baptiste was dead and maybe the woman with the cold cream on her face was right: maybe I *had* caused him to die. And I was to blame for Annabel Lee's experience because I hadn't been smart enough to warn Mr. Jones about the motorcycle fellows. I'd disgraced myself before Charlie and his Happy Timers. The tears kept coming and I didn't try to stop them. I didn't have a job and my money was gone and nobody had laughed at any of my jokes.

I got tired of all my terrible thoughts and huddled there, listening to the speaker, trying to keep my mind a blank.

"And now comes the moment we have all waited for: the dedication of the largest monument ever erected in this city of proud monuments . . ."

I crawled around desperately, wondering how I could escape.

Then the speaker started to give the history of the fund drive and how the money had been raised for the monument, and his voice went on and on, and I was glad that politicians are talkative and like to make long speeches. I looked through the hole and saw the motorcycle fellows again and they were nudging each other and laughing. Rudy grabbed one of them by the arm and shook his head and they quieted down and looked serious again.

The people seemed to be getting restless, a ripple of movement stirring through the crowd, and I hoped they would all get disgusted and go home before the speaker was finished. He showed no signs of stopping. He started to describe all the dimensions of the statue and the base, how tall and broad it was, and he congratulated the women's auxiliaries for pledging to keep fresh flowers all year long in a special flower box at the foot of the statue. I guessed that was the box I was trapped in.

His mention of the flowers must have been some kind of

signal to start the unveiling because a squad of women detached themselves from the crowd and marched, two abreast, toward the platform. They were dressed in white silk dresses and wore blue military hats and carried bouquets of flowers. Two fellows climbed the steps of the platform and disappeared from my view; they must have been standing below me, waiting to pull the ropes that would make the canvas fall away.

"And now," the speaker said, "the good mayor of this fair city will cut the ties that bind the veil and in a moment, ladies and gentlemen, and Honorable Senator and Town Officials and Members of the Clergy, and Soldiers, Sailors and Marines and Veterans of All Wars and members of the United States Air Force who I forgot to mention the first time . . . in a moment we will see a thrilling scene, the noble tribute to our dead war heroes . . ."

The band began to play softly and a shiver rippled through the crowd and everything was still and the fellow who was the mayor walked toward the rear of the platform carrying the biggest pair of scissors I ever saw.

I pulled away from the peephole and sighed. I thought: I'd better stand at attention like everybody else and show them I've got the proper respect, anyway. I stood up and shook away the pain in my temples and brushed off my sports coat and trousers and straightened my honeymoon tie and wet my hand to put my hair in place. I couldn't do anything about the stubble of beard on my face but at least I pushed my shoulders back and drew in my stomach and thought: All right, pull off that canvas and at least I'll make a respectable impression.

It happened so quickly that I was blinded for an instant as the sun exploded in my face, but I kept my arms straight at my sides and my chin rigid, standing at attention the way a soldier does. I didn't move a muscle.

A gasp rose from the crowd as if a huge invisible hand had struck them all a sharp blow across the chest. A silence followed, the kind of silence that is louder than the boom of a cannon, and it gathered itself and spread throughout the square. I almost lost my balance with all that space looming before me and I staggered a bit, losing my nice poise; I had to put one hand against the statue behind me to keep from falling.

Everyone was frozen in the silence, like small toys in a game. I looked up toward the hills and saw the Protestant cemetery far away, the tombstones like aspirin tablets in the sun, and I felt like the only person alive and breathing in the world. The stillness was broken when two policemen sprang to life, waving frantically as they started to run toward the platform. I looked down at the crowd and saw the motorcycle fellows, Rudy at the center of them, a kind of awe on his face, gaping at me in wonder, as if he was some kind of *creator* who could hardly believe what he had done. A fierceness shouted in me, more than anger, more than rage. I felt betrayed, tricked and trapped, stripped down naked before everybody, everything gone, not only my money and my little black book but everything that makes a man what he is, gone now, lost or stolen. I felt like a foolish old man, and the anger thundered in me because I wasn't a foolish old man. I was Tommy Bartin. And I gazed out at the crowd in my fury, the faces raised to me, thousands of them it seemed, some of the people pointing, and they all seemed to be waiting for something to happen.

Damn it, I said to myself, I'll make something happen.

Men were scrambling at the bottom of the base now, lifting a ladder that was painted silver and gold.

And what was I going to make happen? I'd already made enough things happen and I had stood up and disgraced myself in front of the Happy Timers and I thought: There's a time when a man shouldn't do a thing but take his medicine, a time when a man fights back by doing nothing.

I stood at attention, waiting.

Somebody shouted: "Daddyo, hey, daddyo, give us a speech." One of the motorcycle boys.

I raised my hand to wave him away, to make him stop yelling, and as I looked down, the whole world started to spin in front of me, spinning me with it, the square and all the faces rocking and swaying, and I stuck my hand out for support but my hand reached out into nothing and I felt myself swinging off balance, swinging and falling, falling through blank space, the floor of the platform rushing toward me and just before blackness gripped me and swallowed me up, I thought: *You spoiled it all again,* and I wished I would keep plunging, through the wood of the platform and through the grass and into the earth where it was dark and deep and peaceful.

I T'S NICE HERE in the hospital ward. At first I had a bed near the window with a view of the lawn and the highway in the distance but I swapped with an old fellow by the name of John Bolling because he wanted to see the view. He'd pester the nurses to change his place but they were too busy to pay any attention to him. Anyway, we swapped beds, hobbling around the ward one evening when no doctors or nurses were around, and he was as happy as a child on Christmas Eve. Everything was fine until a big male nurse came in later and threw down my sheet and pulled up my johnny and stuck the biggest needle in the world in my buttock and I yelled like a crazy man because it surprised me so much. What happened was that John Bolling and I had forgotten to switch the charts at the foot of our beds. But they let him stay near the window and I was content to be in the middle of the ward because I didn't feel like looking at anything anyway.

Everybody has been very nice. Mr. Jones comes and visits every day and brings Stretch most of the time. Awful Arthur came once, looking raw and thirsty as usual, and he didn't say much, only sniffed the air, smelling the alcohol they use for rubdowns, I guess. Mr. Jones brought Annabel Lee along a few times but there's a hospital rule against children visiting the wards, and she stayed outside. I waved at her from the window and she waved back, getting a big kick out of that, and it was good to see her smiling and happy. She's getting along fine, Mr. Jones says, and that day with the motorcycle fellows has passed away like a bad dream. But I felt a terrible sadness when I waved to her the first time.

Stretch is still the same. He sits by my bed and doesn't say much although he's always asking me if I want a drink of water or need the bedpan. Acting like he's my father, for crying out loud.

My head aches sometimes and the bandages bother me, heavy and tight on my skull, especially on hot days. But I was lucky to escape without any broken bones, the doctor said, although I've got quite a few bruises and my legs hurt once in a while.

I keep thinking of Baptiste. Mr. Jones said that he talked to the police about what happened to Baptiste. He said that last year Baptiste was fished out of Moosock Brook near the Water Street Bridge and told the police he'd slipped and fallen while leaning over the railing.

"But they were suspicious of him all the time, Tommy," Mr. Jones explained. "They figured he'd jumped off. They knew he would probably try again sometime but there was nothing anybody could do. He acted normal enough, too normal to be put away. So it wasn't your fault, what happened to Baptiste. It would have happened sooner or later . . ."

Sometimes I can almost believe that but there are some things a man never knows for sure.

Mr. Jones brought in my wallet last week, the money all gone, but the little card with my social security number still in one of the compartments along with the card asking people to call a priest in case of an accident. But he didn't bring my little black book, and it's still missing.

Later, a policeman stopped in, a young fellow wearing speckle-rimmed glasses, dressed in a neat blue suit as if he was on his way to church. He opened a small pad and spoke like a college professor as he asked me questions. I told him about the young fellows, not because of what they had done to me, but because of those telephone calls they always make. He nodded his head and listened carefully but he didn't take any notes.

"It would be difficult to prove theft of your money," he said, "under the circumstances. To be frank, you might have lost it in your condition, inebriated." He looked at me suddenly and his face softened. "Or possibly sick. The telephone calls are another matter and the telephone company is investigating. But with dial telephones, it's a difficult business. I doubt if anything comes of it. We don't even know the identity of the woman they called." He coughed a little and you could see he was getting restless. "Now, how much would you say your little book was worth?"

I didn't bother answering him. Who can say how much anything is worth? And I thought: Sometime, maybe, when those motorcycle fellows are all grown up and Rudy himself is settled down with a wife and kids, maybe some night the telephone will ring and it will be some *other* young fellow calling up, saying terrible things. Or maybe some fellow will take Rudy's little girl out for a ride. But I felt guilty thinking of that: no one would want that to happen to anybody's child. And I didn't really believe somebody would call him years from now. Things never come out that way.

* * *

A few days ago Mr. Jones asked: "Why did you stay downtown, Tommy? Why didn't you come back after you found out Annie wasn't there?" He was starting to sweat and you could smell that awful deodorant he used. "It was as if you were running away, Tommy . . ."

I thought that over for a long time.

"I wasn't running away from The Place, Mr. Jones," I said. "I thought I was at the time. But I was running away from something else I didn't know about then. Running away from being old, running away from myself . . ."

"You're as young as you feel, Tommy . . ."

"That isn't true, Mr. Jones. Nobody is. I used to believe that and I even wrote it down in my little black book but I don't believe it anymore."

We didn't say anything for a while.

"Well," he said as he stood up to leave, "we've got your room all ready at the infirmary, Tommy. Knobby oiled the barber chair and polished it up . . ."

"That's fine, Mr. Jones," I said. "That's fine . . ."

Yesterday John Bolling and I sat together on the porch. They let him up now because his pneumonia is cured. We watched the breeze bending the rosebuds in the garden. There weren't any more dandelions on the lawn, only pale stems like broken straws, limp after kids get finished with them.

"I'm going home tomorrow maybe," John Bolling said. He's a thin fellow and his blue veins stick out all over him like a road map. "Well, not home exactly. It's one of those nursing homes. They say it's a nice place, with a nice view. My sons, I got two of them, are pitching in to pay for it." He wears false teeth, the old-fashioned kind that never fit right, and they kept clicking away like he had knitting needles in his mouth. "There's some nice people at the place, people my own age. They have a checker tournament every month." He sniffed a little and I hoped he wasn't catching cold. "When you getting out, Tommy?"

"In a few days," I said. "I'm going to have my old room back at the infirmary . . ."

"Do they have checker tournaments?" he asked.

"Not that I know of," I said. "But they got a lot of other things . . ."

"What things?" he asked.

But I didn't know what things to tell him.

What I figure is this:

I'll save my money and it might take quite a while at the rate of eight dollars a month, but I'll give up cigarettes and candy bars, and after a while I'll have a stake. Then I'll go downtown on a regular pass and arrange for a job ahead of time and find a place to live and pay a month in advance. And I won't sign out of The Place permanently until all the arrangements are made.

And I'll act like an old man should, taking it easy, and minding my own business and not expecting people to be interested in me and keeping away from the beer and the nips except on special occasions.

That's what I figure, anyway.

A man can admit that he's seventy years of age but that doesn't mean the sun isn't going to come up tomorrow.